AF447248

# The Spider's Web

Evie Cappelli Book One

By Sophia Beaumont

This is a work of fiction. Names, characters, businesses, places, events and incidents are either the products of the author's imagination or used in a fictitious manner. Any resemblance to actual persons, living or dead, or actual events is purely coincidental.

Copyright © 2016 by Sophia Beaumont

All rights reserved. This book or any portion thereof may not be reproduced or used in any manner whatsoever without the express written permission of the publisher except for the use of brief quotations in a book review.

Printed in the United States of America

First Edition, May 2016.
This edition, March 2024.

ISBN: 979-8-3303-1310-5

For the Tower, and everyone who believed in Evie even
when things looked bleak.

Thank you.

# <u>Prologue</u>
## Footloose and Shoelace Free

They say for a good story to work, you can't ever quit. You have to fight to overcome all obstacles to reach your goal.

The funny thing is, my story began when I gave up.

"I've spent my entire life trying to be like everyone else. I went to Catholic school. I wore the uniforms. I did my best to keep up with the other kids, and to never go past them.

"That's why I like to knit and crochet so much. Every stitch is exactly the same. It's calming. Nothing stands out unless I want it to. I can control the shape it takes, the color, the texture. There's always been someone telling me how to speak, what to wear, how to spend my free time. But this is one thing I control."

Doctor Fisher nodded sagely, eyes closed. The other three members of the group clapped politely. The public speaking portion of the session completed, I relaxed my grip on the slipper I was crocheting ever so slightly.

"Thank you, Evie. You've made some great progress in the past few weeks," she said. Her curly blond hair fought valiantly against the clip binding it in place. One spring-like lock bounced loose and flipped in front of her gaudy glasses. Today's selections were lime green with rhinestones. I swear she had a different pair for every day of the week. Maybe every day of the month.

The doctor checked her watch. "That's all we have time for right now. Same time tomorrow, everyone."

We mumbled our farewells and shuffled off in different directions. I folded up my metal chair and slid it into a corner with the others.

A hand touched my shoulder. "Evie, would you join me in Doctor Sanchez's office?"

I nodded, following Doctor Fisher out of the common room, down the long hallways of St. Mary's.

I'd always thought mental hospitals would have white walls and padded cells. We'd wear uniforms and spend our days on hard leather couches talking about our feelings to doctors with German accents and thick white mustaches.

The reality was a bit different. St. Mary's reminded me of a cross between an elementary school and the office of my childhood pediatrician. Soothing colors with names like Seafoam and Mellow Butter and Clear Skies covered the walls. Patient artwork was taped to the walls. Maybe the adult ward was a little different, but since I was only seventeen, I had to share a ward with kids as young as seven—though there wasn't much overlap in our schedules.

Dr. Fisher buzzed me through the first set of doors to where most of the exam rooms were. Dr. Sanchez, who was in charge of the pediatric ward, had the last office on the left.

"Now this is just preliminary, nothing to worry about, but I think you'll do great. We'll get you back to your family in no time."

"Fantastic." After three months, I was more than

ready to get out. I just wanted my own room with my own things back.

I never could get used to nut house pillows.

I was less sure about going back to my family.

Dr. Sanchez was tall and Latin. He did have a mustache, but it wasn't overly bushy and only beginning to go grey.

"Evie," he boomed. He always boomed when he said our names. "Have a seat." He gestured to the two vinyl-covered chairs across from him.

Dr. Fisher and I each took one while he shuffled his notes.

"I've been hearing good things about you," he said at last. "You've made a lot of progress since you came to us. How do you feel?"

I swallowed, taking a deep breath. "I feel fine." It wasn't a lie. Not really. I felt a lot better. Almost normal, or at least as close to it as I ever got. "I still have my moments, but I understand it's something I'll have to work on, at least for the next few months, if not the rest of my life. There isn't a magic bullet to make depression go away, but I think I've learned how to handle it a bit better now."

He asked me if I looked forward to going home, and what my plans were. I answered as best I could. I dug my fingers into my crocheting, holding it tightly but not stitching. As I'd been reminded many times, it was rude to concentrate on knitting or crochet when someone was speaking to me. I never could understand why. I don't need my eyes to listen, and I don't need my ears to get the stitches right. In fact, I usually don't even have to look at my work at all.

Dr. Sanchez seemed satisfied with my answer. "Yes, we've been concerned about your home life, too. But Dr.

Fisher has been in contact with your family, and they are making adjustments for you."

I hated the way he said it, like they had to rearrange their entire lives because their only daughter couldn't just be *happy* all the time.

"Now, what about your delusions? There was some concern right after you came to us that there was more wrong than just a simple case of chronic depression, at least as simple as it ever is. Any relapses?"

I pointedly didn't look over my shoulder. His hand was there, his attempt to reassure me, such that it was. Average height, curly reddish hair with a streak of silver that matched his eyes, but a face younger than either indicated. I could smell the ozone and leather from his jacket, hear the rustle of his blue jeans when he moved. He'd been there since I woke up in the ICU.

"Just like we rehearsed," he said.

I looked Dr. Sanchez in the eye. "No. None at all."

***

Three months earlier, when I woke up in the hospital, groggy and sore, my hands still partially numb after the rough incisions I'd made in my wrists with a butcher knife, it wasn't my mom and dad who were waiting for me.

Uncle Mike had a day's growth of beard and deep shadows under his eyes. One hand partially obscured his face, but he was the picture of misery.

On my other side, his younger sister, Izzy, squeezed my hand and leaned forward at the first signs of life. "Evie? Are you awake, honey?" she asked.

At first I was confused. "What are you doing here?" I croaked through dry lips. "You're supposed to be in

Montreal."

"I drove down right away when I heard what happened," she said. There were tears in her eyes as she stroked my hair.

Across from her, my strong, fun-loving, police detective uncle didn't say a word, merely dissolved into tears and clutched my hand.

I didn't know what to say or do. I was still a little out of it. Half a bottle of night-time pain killers and massive blood loss will do that, I guess.

I spent a couple of days in intensive care before being sent to the psych ward. At first, they thought the people I kept seeing in my room were an after-effect of all the medications and the trauma. There was the guy with the shredded left side, who looked like he'd been hit by a car. He wandered up and down the hallway at night, howling for someone named Betty, but she never answered. And then there was the lady in the old-fashioned, pink striped uniform with the little cap, who kept coming in and offering me cigarettes and candy. She was nice enough, but a little weird. She kept talking about soldiers. But she kept most of the others out of my room, which was good.

That just left the one with the silver eyes. He watched me patiently from the corner, looking as wrung out as Uncle Mike. Unlike the others, he didn't leave. Sometimes I couldn't see him, but I still knew he was there.

"You can't tell them I'm here. That any of us are here," he warned, after I'd asked Mike and Izzy for the umpteenth time who the weird guy in my room was. "They can't see us. They'll lock you up for good if you keep asking questions."

Slowly, I learned. I adjusted to the rhythm of the hospital and then the ward. I learned not to flinch when the maimed or out-of-place walked by, sometimes walking straight through walls or even other people. I learned to look at the floor when I walked so I wouldn't see them, and not to listen to the snatches of conversation, the pleas, the cries of pain all around me.

I learned what to say and how to say it.

And the whole time, I stitched like crazy, uncertain if I was more afraid to stay or go.

Knitting helped keep me calm through my three-month stay at St. Mary's. Finally, Dr. Sanchez decided I could go home the last week of March. Once the doctors made their decision, things moved quickly.

Home was just as inhospitable as I remembered. My parents barely knew what to do with me when I was sane, let alone when I was straight out of the psych ward. We fought constantly, and when we weren't fighting, I was invisible.

It was just like before. The blackness crept over me again within hours.

I lay on my bed, hugging my pillow and trying to ignore the specter on the other side of the room. I wondered at the wisdom of keeping him to myself. If I'd told the doctors, they would have kept me longer. They would have put me on even more pills, they'd have had even worse side effects, and there was no promise they would even work.

But I was good at ignoring him. Ignoring, I could do. And it seemed to be working.

I hugged my pillow as tightly as I could. *You need to get up. You need to do something. You can't just sit here and wallow like a baby. You're too old for this.* All of my affirmations floated out of my mind when faced with the disappointed, angry look on my mother's face.

He rested his hand on mine. "Evie, you are not too

old. You are not wallowing."

I peered at him around the pillowcase.

He gave me a lopsided smile. "Well, maybe a little. It's not wrong for you to come home and want understanding. You're not out of line in wanting them to care for you. You need to stand on your own, sure, but you also need to ask for help every once in a while."

I buried my head back into the pillow. "What do you know? I am not taking psychiatric advice from a hallucination."

He sighed. "I'm not a hallucination. And that wasn't advice, that was fact. If you want advice, here's some: Get the hell out. You shouldn't be here. You should be anywhere *but* here. This place is toxic. Find someplace, anyplace, where you'll be safe."

Right. Where was I going to go? I'd barely made it out of high school, and I was unemployed. I didn't have any friends I could stay with long term, and there was no way I could pay rent. Staying with one of my multitude of relatives would be even worse. The only one I was really close to was Uncle Mike, but he had enough on his plate. And after…well, I just couldn't. I couldn't do that to him.

"Izzy."

I looked at him over the pillow again.

"Ask to stay with Izzy. She'll say yes. And a change in scenery will do you good."

So that was how I wound up moving five hundred kilometers to Montreal.

# Chapter One
## Coming Out of My Shell

*June, 2010*
*Montreal, QC*

"If I get one more report like this, you're out of here, Cappelli. I don't have the time or money to waste on dead weight!" Caroline snapped.

She held her office door open for me, and I slunk out, eyes glued to my Converse.

"The only thing standing between Periwinkle Books and bankruptcy is the fact that we have the highest customer service scores in the industry. I will not keep you around if you're going to jeopardize that."

"Yes, ma'am," I mumbled. *I will not cry in public, I will not cry in public...*

My constant companion looked almost as livid as my boss. He stood toe to toe with her, shouting impotently. "Listen, you bitch, she didn't do anything—"

I nodded swiftly and practically ran out of the office.

"I can't believe it. That woman was an absolute idiot, and then to blame you—"

"Can you please stop talking now?" I said under my breath, praying no one heard me talking to myself. "It's really distracting."

Micha huffed, eyes blazing. "I'm sorry. I just—That was so uncalled for! She—"

The sales floor was busy, but not overly so. I managed to make it to the back room, where I loaded a box of new arrivals onto a flatbed and wheeled it out.

I ducked down behind a display of poetry, one of the least shopped departments in the entire store, and pretended to straighten already perfect shelves so no one would see my eyes going misty. I'd worked hard to keep up with my treatments—taking my medications, going to counseling, doing all of the little things I was supposed to.

But some days I still woke up feeling about as tough as spun sugar. Today was one of those days.

*I can't handle this right now. I just want them to leave me alone. Why can't they leave me alone?* I wiped my eyes on a sleeve. Even though we weren't busy, it still felt like there were too many people in the store, pressing in all around me. I knew if they saw me, they would start to talk. They would whisper about me, the weird girl, the one who couldn't hack it, the one who never did anything right—

"Excuse me, can you tell me where psychology is?"

The words jerked me forcibly from my thoughts. I hoped my eyes weren't too red.

I blinked at him a few times. I was still kneeling on the floor, and the customer, who was tall and skinny, looked over me, confused.

"Psychology."

"Yeah."

"You mean like self-help?"

"No, like text books."

I nodded. "Second floor. It's on the left, after… Just

follow me," I said, hauling myself to my feet with an effort. I felt my joints pop like I was seventy instead of seventeen.

*Well isn't this ironic.* Asking the head case where the books on psychology were. That's a new one.

My brain darted off in a dozen different directions as I led him to the stairs. *He's cute. Why couldn't he leave me alone? He only asked me because he can tell I'm nuts, right? Is this some kind of sick joke? Did I put on deodorant this morning?* I realized with horror the answer was no. Where was my head? What was I thinking? *Not like he'd be interested anyway. Why am I even thinking about this? I'm supposed to be working. I might not have a job much longer. Oh, god. What will I do if I get fired? Don't worry about it. There's nothing more you can do. I can do better. I'm never going to find another job. Is he looking at me? Can he tell I forgot deodorant?*

Too wrapped up in my own head, I almost led him straight past psychology and into history. "Right here. Is there a specific title you're looking for?"

He gave me a measuring look, then pulled out a list. "Yeah, I need these for a summer class." There were three books on the list. I'd skimmed most of that section after I came to Montreal, trying to figure out what was going on my head. Most psychology books just made me angry. The entire basis of the field was that everyone had something wrong with them, but I couldn't find what was wrong with me. Of course, my spectral companion was no help, and kept insisting I wasn't crazy.

The redhead in question let out a long-suffering sigh. "You know, 'specter' is a misnomer. I'm not a ghost. Or a hallucination. I'm a spirit. How many times do I have to keep telling you that?"

"Get out of my head," I mumbled, flicking the first title off the shelf.

"Excuse me?"

"Sorry, not you," I said to the customer, my face heating. "It looks like we only have the second one in French. Is that okay?"

He huffed out a thoughtful breath of air. "Can I order it in English? My French really isn't that great." His accent was British Columbian, not Quebec.

"I'll check. It usually takes about a week."

"Okay."

"I'll have to order the last one, too. Doesn't look like it's in stock."

"That's fine."

I led him over to the computer terminal and started typing in the titles. He stood next to me, extremely close. I concentrated on the computer screen.

"Okay, so *Introduction to Human Psychology* will be here on Monday, but *Human Psyche* is on backorder, and it's estimated thirty days for delivery."

"Shit. I need that one for a summer class."

"We do have an e-book edition, which is half-price." I pointed to the screen. "You can read it on your phone." I clicked the link. "The e-book is also updated and includes links to other resources." I tapped my finger nervously on the keyboard rest. I'd already been chewed out once for telling someone we didn't have their book in stock. *Don't be mad, don't be mad. I can't fix it.*

He reached across me for the mouse and his hand brushed mine. He hesitated, then turned to look at me.

"It's okay, really. It's going to be okay."

I pulled back. "What?"

"Sorry. I just mean, you don't have to worry. It's going to come out all right. It always does."

Somehow, I knew he wasn't talking about the e-book versus hard copy debate. "I don't know what you're talking about." I felt the spun sugar inside me snap. I turned and walked quickly away before I fell apart.

I had no idea when my break was supposed to be, but I took it anyway. I practically ran out of the store, down the stairs, into the lower levels of the mall. It was too damn crowded, too noisy. There was no place to escape.

I ducked into a bathroom. It was blessedly empty. No one came down the north corridor much, thanks to the remodel that had closed the nearest anchor store for a month. I locked myself in a stall, practically hyperventilating.

"You don't have to worry. He wouldn't have hurt you," my hallucination said from the other side of the stall door. Through the gap underneath, I could see his Birkenstocks and the frayed hem of his jeans.

"Go away. Why are you even here?" I asked, pressing the heels of my hands into my eyes. I sat down on the edge of the toilet, trying to breathe deeply and tame the anxiety I'd been fighting. It sucks to have anxiety and depression; one gives this wild energy where you have to get up and do things and feel like you've accomplished something, a need for control, while the other just wants to hide in a closet and not face anything.

I spent a lot of time pacing my room in circles before I went to St. Mary's.

"I'm here because you need me."

"Yeah, you keep saying that. But I'm pretty sure I don't need to be hallucinating."

When I looked up again, he was in the stall with me, kneeling at my feet. It could barely contain us both.

He took my hand. His fingers were cold and calloused.

"You know, at first I wasn't even sure you could see me. I've been with you forever, but you've never really noticed."

*I'll give him one thing, he has a soothing voice.*

He pushed back my sleeve and ran his fingers over my scars. "I know I've caused you some trouble, and I don't mean to. I really am just here to help. The only thing in this world I want is for you to find happiness."

When he looked at me, I saw a sadness that matched my own. A special kind of loneliness which comes from always being around people but never being part of the group.

"I'm here to back you up. No matter what happens, I'll be here to listen if you need it. That's my job. But for you to get better, you need to get back out there. You can't spend your life hiding in bathrooms." His thumb found my cheekbone and a stray tear there, wiping it away. "You can be strong, Evie. Stronger than you know. You've already overcome so much. One customer in a stupid little book store? That's nothing. You're destined to fight dragons much bigger than that, and I know you can do it."

He rose, pulling me up with him. On a whim, I stepped in and laid my head on his shoulder, just for a second. He rested his hands on my upper arms, but it was more of a hug than I'd gotten in a long time.

I shivered. "You're cold."

"Spirit. Sorry. See, if I were a hallucination, I'd feel like a real person, now wouldn't I?"

"What's your name?" He'd been following me around for months, but I'd never asked.

"Micha."

"Micha." I tested it out. Then I took a deep breath and stepped back. "Okay. I should get back to work now."

"Attagirl."

I thought of the store. The people. "Do I have to?"

"You'll do fine."

I took a deep breath, and with great force of will, unlocked the stall.

I went back to my cart of books to find a massive, long-legged spider waiting for me.

It looked at me.

I looked at it.

It took two steps toward me—or would that be sixteen, with all those legs?

I squished it with a volume of Poe.

"Alas, nevermore," I said, sliding it discreetly back onto the shelf.

I'd nearly finished unloading the books, and was on my way back to the stockroom when someone stopped me.

"Hey."

I jumped and spun around. It was the cute psychology guy.

"Sorry, I didn't mean to scare you."

"No, it's not your fault. I—I've been having a bad day. I'm sorry I freaked out on you."

"It's okay. I know. I mean, I'm good at reading people. Sometimes I just say more than I should. I didn't mean to embarrass you or anything."

"Don't worry about it. I overreacted." I brushed my hair behind my ear, twisting my finger in the strands. Damn it, I always played with my hair when I was nervous. I dropped my arm quickly to my side.

He nodded, but didn't walk away. "I'm not trying to be creepy or weird or anything, but if you want to talk…."

I raised an eyebrow. "Is this homework or something?

Diagnosing random strangers?”

"No! Nothing like that. I just mean… You seem to be in a rough place. I like listening. I'd like to help if I can."

My automatic response was to say no, but part of my treatment involved not shutting people out just because they were nice to me.

"…Okay?"

He handed me a half sheet of notebook paper with his name and phone number on it: *Adam Gold*. "I'll see you around. Maybe we can get coffee or something."

"Yeah. Okay. Sure."

# Chapter Two
# The Kill-It-'Til-It-Dies Two Step

In all honesty, Aunt Izzy didn't have any more clue what to do with me than my parents, but she was at least willing to try. She didn't spend all her time telling me what I should and shouldn't do or freaking out if I was alone for five minutes, though she always looked relieved afterward. She always offered an ear, but was willing to give me space when I needed it, which was almost always.

That night, Izzy went out to celebrate a friend's birthday. She said she'd be back by ten.

I told her not to worry. I had my knitting, and the first five chapters of her new manuscript to read. Once my ass hit the couch, I wasn't planning to move for anything

With a pint of moose tracks ice cream, a pair of socks, and the printout, I flopped down on her blue leather sofa and prepared for an indulgent evening alone.

Well, except for Micha. But I let him have the remote and Izzy's chair, and there was a *Firefly* marathon on, so he was happy with his space cowboys.

Or I thought he was.

"Please stop staring at me."

"Sorry." He turned back to the television.

I scrawled an "s" on the page, since I was pretty sure that even in Izzy's fantasy world pies weren't hung for their crimes. "You're staring again."

"Sorry. I can't help it."

"What are you, some kind of supernatural stalker?" He'd barely been out of sight for longer than it took me to go to the bathroom since I'd woken up in the hospital.

The look he gave me was less than kind. "I'm your guardian spirit. It's my job to watch over you."

"All the time?"

"Yes."

"Can't you do something else?"

"Not really. I've got a range, but… You know, you weren't so bothered by it when you first started seeing me."

"That's because I was ignoring you because I thought I was crazy and I was more concerned with an impending mental breakdown."

"You still think you're crazy."

"Yes, but I'm starting to make peace with it."

"Which, in a way, means you're not crazy. Probably."

"You're not very helpful."

"I'm very helpful. You just don't appreciate my many talents."

"Like what, channel surfing?"

Micha gave a sniff of mock offense. "Just because you don't appreciate Joss Whedon doesn't mean the rest of us are lacking taste."

"Really. And what about all that late night TV you watch? I know Izzy isn't the one watching *Star Trek* and old Judy Garland movies at three in the morning."

"Hey, the best stuff is on after midnight."

"Right. So how was the infomercial for the Chop-O-Matic last night?"

"It was the Super Chop-O-Matic, for your information, and it was surprisingly entertaining. Besides, what else am I going to do while you're asleep?"

I rolled my eyes and went back to my sock and my reading, but Micha was now officially ignoring the adventures of the Serenity and her crew.

"Stop it."

"Stop what?"

"You're grinning at me."

"I'm smiling. And contrary to what you seem to believe, a smile does not make a person untrustworthy."

"Whatever. Why are you smiling at me like a crazy person?"

He shrugged. "Well, you're talking to—"

"Gah!" I threw down my knitting, swatting at the back of my neck.

"What? What is it?" Micha demanded. In an instant he was right beside me.

"Something bit me!" I tiny legs scampered over my skin. I brushed it off, flipping my hair over my head to shake it out.

A hairy, black spider the size of a nickel landed on the hardwood floor. I screamed and stomped on it with my flip-flop.

"What is going on with these stupid spiders? They're all over the place!" At work, at home—I touched the back of my neck, where a welt was already forming. I ran to the bathroom and used Izzy's compact to try to get a better look at it in the vanity mirror. "You don't think that's poisonous or anything, do you?"

"Venomous. And I think it's worse than that," Micha

said, his eyes on the floor.

I looked down. From a tiny gap where the baseboard met the floor, a line of spiders emerged. I screamed and stomped on them. But then there were more—from under the cupboard, behind the medicine chest. In through the window. From every crevice they came, and my dollar store sandals couldn't keep up.

"I'm crazy now, right? Please tell me this is a hallucination!" I cried, stumbling out of the bathroom. There were more in the hallway, crawling down the walls and out from under the carpet. They swarmed over my feet, landed on my arms. They bit faster than I could brush them away.

A sudden burst of light from my left, and a chunk of the spiders vanished.

"Evie! They're not real! They're constructs!"

"Idon'tknowwhatthatmeansbutmakethemgoaway." Sobbing hysterically was a good response, right?

"Concentrate! They're made of spiritual energy, just like me. You can make them go away!"

I was in tears by that point. Itchy red sores covered my skin. I could hardly breathe, but I couldn't tell if it was from panic or the bites.

Another burst of light, but it wasn't enough. They just kept coming.

Micha stepped in front of me and grabbed my arms. "Evie! Look at me!"

Silver-grey eyes filled my vision.

"You have to calm down. You can do this. Just picture a circle of white light all around you. Nothing can get past."

"I can't— I can't—!"

"You can! Now listen to me!" He gave me a shake, just once, just hard enough to get my attention.

I squeezed my eyes shut and tried to do what he said.

"Are you picturing it? Now put everything you've got into it!"

Tiny legs, all over me. Biting, eating away at my whole body. Under my clothes. In my ears, my mouth—

*I can't—I can't—just—* "GO AWAY!"

The shrill scream tore from my throat. Something in my head shattered and I went weak-kneed, leaning on Micha. When I opened my eyes, they were gone. I was left exhausted, with only a few bites on my arms and legs.

"I thought you said they weren't real," I said, cringing at a particularly nasty looking one.

"Most of them weren't. I think there must have been a few, just nearby ones that answered the call, but most of them were just…an illusion, for lack of a better word. A very powerful illusion." He pushed my hair back from my face. He looked as relieved as I felt.

"What was that? Why were they here?" Dammit, I was going to start crying again. I'd already done too much of that today.

"I don't know. But they're gone now. We'll find a way to keep them from coming back."

I shook all over. "I need a shower. And bug spray. Lots and lots of bug spray."

Micha started to object, but closed his mouth.

I looked over his shoulder into the bathroom. "Not that shower." Izzy would have to forgive me for using the master bath just this once. There was no way I was taking off my clothes in there. In fact, I might never be able to use it again, for anything.

***

Once I was showered and at least resembling a sane human again—though there was still a twitch above my right eye that I feared might be permanent—I grabbed my purse and headed for the front door. It was getting late, but the dépanneur at the end of the street would still be open. I just hoped they had industrial sized cans of Raid.

Micha, as always, trailed along beside me. He seemed to be deep in thought and I was still jumping at shadows, so we didn't talk much for the first block or two.

Izzy lived in an affluent part of Montreal called Outremont. Just north of Mount Royal, it was as close as you could get to the Mountain without living in the cemetery at its base. Outremont was full of brick and stone row houses, and pristine Victorians with actual yards surrounded by huge maple and oak trees. Izzy's place was actually a duplex; one of those Victorians chopped up into apartments. Izzy had the top floor, and technically the attic, but as far as I knew the only thing she used it for was storing out of season clothes and the stuff she was too lazy to put in the yard sale she always claimed she was going to have, but never got around to.

Anyway, Outremont was a quiet neighborhood. Lots of older residents and families, and a lot of immigrants and second- or third-generation Canadians. During daylight hours, you were as likely to hear German, Russian, and Yiddish on the street as you were the standard English and French. One of the draws of Outremont was it also had the largest percentage of Anglophones on the island, which I guess was the reason Izzy picked it. My French was good, but not great, and even I flinched every time she had to order a pizza or ask for directions. She had the vocabulary, but her accent would make anyone who had ever heard the language cringe.

The quiet neighborhood pretty much shut down after dark unless it was a holiday, so I was wary when I spotted a figure coming toward me. It wasn't quite dark enough for the street lamps to come on, but I could tell it was a man.

Instantly, I was on high alert. I walked faster and considered crossing the street. With my nerves still completely fried, everything was a threat. He was walking toward me, and that could only mean one thing—

"Evie, calm down." Micha's hand brushed mine.

I sucked in a breath—

"Hey! It's you again!" The figure waved, a huge grin splitting his shadowed face. A few more steps, and he passed into the last vestiges of sunlight as they vanished behind the trees.

I stopped, completely aghast. It was psychology boy.

"God, you must think I'm following you or something. I swear I'm not. But three times in one day? That's gotta be fate or something, right?" His eyes crinkled when he smiled. He had big brown eyes, like one of those giant dogs that looks like it could swallow you whole but would rather curl up in your lap all night. His long, curly dark ponytail made me think of a poodle at first, which made me snort in an attempt not to laugh. I tried to turn it into a cough, but somehow Micha must have caught the image because then he started laughing— and then I sounded like I was dying because I was trying not to picture Adam Gold with a poodle's butt on his head.

"Are you…okay?" he asked, sounding like he was rethinking his position on my sanity. Again.

"Yeah. I'm fine. Really." I turned slightly so I couldn't see Micha. He had the good sense to stay out of view. "So, what are you doing here?"

"Oh, I live just down this way, near the university. Just on my way home from work." He gestured at his red polyester vest, his name written on a piece of masking tape on the left breast.

"You haven't worked there long, have you?"

"How can you tell? It's the name tag, isn't it?"

"No. I'm in Chan's all the time, and I've never seen you."

"I just started this week. Trying to get a head start on a summer job."

I'd almost forgotten it was June, and classes would be letting out in two weeks. Nine months ago, I'd just been starting at the University of Toronto.

I shuddered at the memory. I didn't want to think about nine months ago.

Despite my paranoia, once I started talking to Adam, I realized he was probably the most non-threatening person I'd ever met. He exuded such a laid-back, calm attitude that it was impossible not to relax at least a little in his company. He put me at ease. Oddly enough, Micha did almost the exact same thing, but in a different way.

Still, I couldn't shake the feeling of someone watching us. The hair on the back of my sore neck stood at attention, and I felt eyes boring into my back.

"Is something wrong?" Adam asked, catching my discomfort.

"I—I'm fine," I said.

"Do you want me to walk with you?"

I held back, then consented. "If you wouldn't mind. I'm not going far. Just to the dep."

"Making me go back to work already." He sighed theatrically.

Something rustled behind us and I jumped. "Sorry.

I'm a little wound up tonight, I guess."

"No worries. It was probably just a raccoon or something." Adam offered me his arm, my knight in shining polyester.

I could practically feel Micha rolling his eyes behind me, and shot him a look over my shoulder.

"What's wrong with you?" I mouthed.

He shook his head and didn't respond.

Adam and I chatted as we continued our journey. Or rather, he talked and I listened. I learned he was originally from a small town a little outside of Vancouver, but had moved to Montreal in high school because of his dad's job. He was actually going to McGill to study psychology, but the duplex he shared with three other students was nearby. Outremont was adjacent to the Université de Montréal, and there was a lot of student housing along the fringes, especially farther west. Izzy's place was right on the edge, and I suspected it was the reason she could afford to live there.

The feeling didn't go away. I tried to tell myself to be calm, I was imagining things, but when I looked back I saw Micha appeared on edge, too, and was also looking behind us.

"So you're not a Quebecer, either, are you?" Adam asked, politely ignoring my anxiety. Or maybe trying to distract me from it.

"Um, no. I just came out here a few months ago. I've been living with my aunt."

"Do you go to school here?"

"No." Damn, I was one hell of a conversationalist, wasn't I? No wonder I'd made so many friends in Montreal.

If Adam intended to continue his line of questioning, I didn't find out because the next second something flew at my head.

I threw myself on the ground, taking Adam with me. "What the hell?"

The thing came back for a second round—an owl. An enormous brown owl with huge, glowing golden eyes. It dove straight at my face with a screech, claws catching in my hair and tearing out a chunk.

I screamed. Blood coated my fingertips when I touched my scalp.

Adam took off his vest and tried to swat at it, but it was ineffectual. The bird came around a third time, claws extended.

Gripping the long strap of my purse, I swung up at it and missed. I tried to summon the light I had used in the bathroom, but I couldn't. It was moving too fast and if I stopped to think, it would get us.

A second bird joined the first.

"What is wrong with the animals here?" I shouted, taking a swing at the newcomer. "Micha!"

"I can't do anything. Those are real birds," he said, watching helplessly from the sidelines. He tried to shoo them away, but was about as effective as a *no smoking* sign in a Montreal café. One of the birds snapped at him, but its beak passed through his hand like it wasn't even there.

My purse finally connected with one of them, knocking it, dazed, to the sidewalk. The other was apparently trying to pull out Adam's eyes.

"Come on!" I grabbed his arm and dragged him to his feet, setting off at a run in any direction that didn't involve a psychotic owl.

I can only imagine how we must have looked to anyone who happened to peer out their window at that moment. A couple running from a pair—and then a *trio*—of owls on an otherwise quiet street in one of the biggest cities in North America.

With no thought for direction or destination, I ran as fast as I could. Once he had his balance, Adam easily could have outrun me, but instead he grabbed my hand, pulling me along with him. I stumbled, trying to match his longer strides.

My arms, already covered in at least half a dozen spider bites, had been torn open by claws and beaks. I could hardly see where I was going from the wings beating in my face.

I managed another good hit with my purse and broke free from the birds. I bolted, running flat out for several meters. I spared a second to glance back over my shoulder to see if they were following, and landed face first on grass.

A low growl emanated from somewhere in the vicinity. I covered my head, pressing myself to the ground as best I could.

The owls shrieked; a dog snarled and Adam shouted. I rolled over in time to see him stumbling through the fence, collapsing on the thick, grassy lawn of Mount Royal Cemetery.

At the gate, an enormous black dog growled and pounced, taking one of the birds from the air and tearing it to shreds in a matter of moments. The other two fled.

Adam lay, panting, on his back, barely a meter from the dog, who was making quick work of its prey. He crawled backward, catching sight of me.

I froze, crouched behind a tombstone.

Deciding the dog was suitably occupied, Adam scrambled to his feet and joined me.

"Could this night get any weirder?" I wondered, partially to myself and partially to the world at large.

"I don't know, but we need to get out of here," Adam said. He clutched my arm. I wasn't sure if it was a protective gesture, or if he was simply as scared as I was.

Belching feathers, the dog finished with its snack and turned in our direction.

"Do you think we can outrun it?" he whispered.

It was a really, really big dog. At least waist high on me, and I'm above average height for most women.

"I doubt it."

"Don't worry," Micha said. "It won't hurt you."

"Don't tell me it's not a real dog!" I snapped. There was no way—if it wasn't real, how had it eaten the bird?

"Why would I tell you it's not real?" Adam asked, panic in his voice.

*Great,* now *he figures out I'm crazy.* "I wasn't talking to you!"

The dog yawned and trotted over to us like nothing was wrong.

Adam and I stood frozen, afraid moving would incur its wrath, but we needn't have worried. It walked straight up to Micha, bumping his hand with its enormous head. Micha obliged by scratching behind the floppy ears. The dog's tail and back leg twitched happily.

Adam dropped my arm, backing away. His eyes were the size of dinner plates, and he was staring directly at Micha. "What—Who—GHOST!"

"Adam, look out!"

His knees caught on the back of a low headstone, and he flipped backward over the marker.

"Are you okay?" I stood over him. He lay panting on the ground. I could almost see little animated stars dancing around his head.

"I thought…there was a ghost. I swear. I thought I saw someone. This guy in a leather jacket…"

I glanced over a Micha. He looked the same to me, just as real as always. "You can see him?"

Adam's mouth worked. He looked ridiculous, with his legs still draped over the headstone. Micha joined us. When he saw Micha and the dog, Adam tried to get up but a vicious wreath tied him down. He shook his leg in a vain attempt to get it off. He did succeed in knocking over a little vase of flowers, however, and cracked his shin against the stone marker so hard I winced.

"I won't hurt you." With one hand on the dog's head, Micha placed a hand on Adam's shoulder.

I thought he would start screaming again, but my new friend just took a deep breath and slowly sat up, pulling flowers off his ankles.

"You can see him. You can really see him?" I asked, kneeling beside Adam. If Adam could see him, then it meant I wasn't nuts, right?

"Yeah, I can see him."

Micha smiled at us, patting the dog's head. "Like I tried to tell you earlier, this dog won't hurt you. She belongs to Hekate, the keeper of the spirit realm. That's why you can see me," he said, nodding to Adam. "She's a link between this world and the next. We're in her territory right now." He gestured at the graveyard.

"Who…who are you?" Adam stuttered, still wary.

"My name is Micha. I'm…I'm a friend of Evie's."

Adam looked at me for clarification.

"It's a long story." Yeah, not so much on the clarification at the moment.

"So you're like a ghost, then?"

"Kind of." I could see him making an effort not to give Adam the same exasperated speech I'd had to sit through so many times. "I'm a spirit. It's like being a ghost, except I was never alive. I'm a guardian."

Adam still looked confused and more than a little terrified.

"He won't hurt you," I said. "He's been following me around for months and he's never done anything bad. He's just a little annoying."

"Hey!"

"Well, you are."

Adam nodded. "Okay. Spirits. Ghosts. Okay. Not what I was expecting." He took another deep breath.

I put a hand on his arm.

"Can you please not do that right now?" he said, pulling away slightly.

I'll admit, I was kind of hurt. Here I was trying to help, and he brushed me off.

Micha looked at me, giving an almost unperceivable shake of his head. Between us, Adam covered his face with his hands, taking long, slow breaths. I leaned back to let him have some space.

"It's nothing to be frightened of," Micha said. "You knew I was here all along."

Before I could ask how that was even possible, Adam nodded. "Yeah, but seeing and sensing are two different things."

I raised my hand. "I'm confused."

"Adam is an empath." Micha said it like it was most obvious thing in the world. "You're not the only one with special abilities."

"I do not—" Okay, there had been the thing with the spiders. I hadn't really been able to process that yet.

*We are having a major talk when we get home.*

Home.

Izzy.

*Shit.*

# Chapter Three
## Evie, Warrior Priestess

Micha and I did not have time for a chat that evening. I felt bad abandoning Adam after everything that had happened, so I wound up walking him home instead. It was nice to know I wasn't crazy, though once we left the security of the cemetery and the protection of Hekate's dog, Micha became invisible to everyone but me again.

The evening left me with dozens of questions, and Adam had even more. He asked several on the walk to his house, but I couldn't answer most of them, at least not yet, and Micha didn't seem to know the answers, either.

At home, Izzy waited in the living room. She was in her chair with the edgy look which meant she'd been panicking privately and trying not to show it.

"Where did you go?" she asked oh-so-casually.

"We needed bug spray."

"And you had to go out in the middle of the night?"

"This isn't the middle of the night. It's not even eleven." Experience with my mother made me sense an oncoming third degree. I had no idea how long I'd been gone or how long she'd been back, and I had nothing to show for the outing except dirt on my jeans and scrapes on the palms of my hands from tripping over the grave marker. I hid them behind my back and hoped she wouldn't notice my jeans in the low lighting of the hallway.

Izzy opened her mouth, then closed it, giving me a once over. "You're okay?"

"Peachy."

Her mouth twisted slightly. "Okay. But if you're going to be out late like that again, leave a note or something, 'kay?"

I meant to grill Micha with the same intensity my mom would have used to grill me, but as soon as I sat down on the bed, I realized how exhausted I was. The next thing I knew, Izzy was knocking on my door, reminding me of a doctor's appointment I was about to be late for. I cracked one eye open to discover I was on top of the covers, still fully clothed except for one sandal.

9:48 am.

Swearing, I rolled out of bed and landed with a thud on the rug. I grabbed a pair of slightly less filthy jeans from the pile at the bottom of my closet.

"Bag," Micha said as I headed for the door.

"Shit. Izzy! Car, please!"

With my ratty tote bag over one shoulder, I raced into the hall, using the doorframe as a pivot.

"No parking tickets!" Izzy hollered from her office when she heard me grab the keys. "And remember to put gas in her this time!"

"Thank you!"

Driving in Montreal is only marginally faster than using public transit, but that's mostly because it takes so long to find a parking space. Finding one that doesn't cost an arm and a leg is even more difficult. Throw Izzy's ancient Jeep into the mix, it's a recipe for disaster, but I was late enough that waiting for the bus was out of the question.

Seldom run, the Jeep made an awful squealing noise when I started it, and stalled as I backed onto the street. A bright red Honda honked as it swerved, narrowly missing the Jeep's rear bumper, leaving a string of French sacres in its wake.

Twisting the key and pumping the accelerator, I managed to start the car again, and chugged off in the direction of downtown.

Anyone planning to drive in Montreal at any point in the future might want to think twice.  I saw more traffic violations by the time I reached the end of the Izzy's street than most highway patrolmen do in a month, and that's not even counting the woman who drove backwards down the neighboring one-way street every morning on her way to work.

Mount Royal is practically sacred to most of the locals. So sacred, in fact, that for many years no roads could be built on the hill itself, which rises up in the center of the island, casting its shadow over the city center when viewed from the southeast. At least until Camillien Houde, a former member of parliament and mayor of Montreal, died. He'd been really big on protecting the Mountain.

So one of his successors had a road built and named after him.

The Quebecois are contrary like that.

Unfortunately, that road ran in the opposite direction I needed to be going, so I had no choice but to drive the long way around the north end of the mountain, take Pine Avenue south again, and then make a big circle up to Dr. Penfield Avenue.

A stone's throw from Montreal General Hospital, the Pine-Penfield loop is filled with independent practices, mostly of the psychological nature, which the hospital outsources a lot of its patients to. While Canada provides great health coverage, Quebec once again decided to be contrary and omitted psychiatric care from the list of covered treatments. With a few exceptions, most of the shrinks in the city ran private practices from the multitude of row houses in the more affluent neighborhoods, with the Westmount-Golden Square Mile-Shaughnessy Village area chief among them.

Of course, that part of town is also one of the hardest to park in.

The Jeep shuddered to a stop in a rare street-side space, a dozen meters from Dr. Archambault's front door. Only slightly crooked and with no chance of restarting the car without a major incident, I called it a win, grabbed my bag, and raced up the sidewalk to the door, punching the button by his name with my thumb.

I was panting by the time I reached his office on the third floor. His secretary, a grey haired woman in cat-eyed glasses I'm pretty sure were authentic to the '50s, glared at me over her magazine. "Vous êtes en retard," she said shortly, pushing a button on the intercom with one pointy, manicured finger. From a spot near her shoulder, a rhinestone pin in the shape of a spider winked at me. I shuddered.

"Sorry," I gasped. I slumped a man in a suit reading the paper and slipped through the wooden door separating reception from Dr. Archambault's lair. While the receptionist was distracted by her magazine, I shot Micha a warning look. The last thing I needed was for my shrink to catch me talking to my invisible friend.

In a stark contrast from the aggressively calming colors which had surrounded me at St. Mary's, and Dr. Fisher's perpetually perky disposition and flamboyant spectacle choices, Dr. A's office looked like something out of a documentary about Freud. Heavy, dark wood shelves lined the walls of the turn-of-the-century home-turned-office. A massive mahogany desk—almost as old as the building—stood framed by a bay window, and flanked on either side by a ficus. A red velvet couch, worn almost threadbare, and more diplomas than you could shake a stick at, rounded out the decor.

The good doctor himself only came up to my eyebrows, and his dark hair was rapidly going white. Bushy white eyebrows tried to hide behind thick bifocals. He always showed up at the office in a three piece suit, usually grey pinstripes, but if the photos on the bookcases were any indication, he'd rather be in waders and flannel somewhere along the St. Laurence or its many tributaries. The man himself was unassuming, but the office screamed old world masculine power.

"Ah, Evie. How good of you to join us."

I looked around. Except for Dr. A, the room was empty.

"Sorry. I…had an issue."

"Oh? Would you care to elaborate?"

"I overslept." I felt like I was back in homeroom. Now, where was my homework, and what was the test supposed to be about? Oh, right. The tenuous status of my mental health.

"Long night?" When he smiled, his eyes crinkled until his brows resembled a living thing, threatening to consume the orbits wholesale. The effect made him seem less the rigid doctor, and more the friendly old grandpa. He reminded me of my grandpa, a little, except Grandpa usually hid behind a newspaper instead of asking questions. He generally just agreed with whatever Grandma told him his opinion was.

I realized belatedly that I hadn't brushed my long,

dark hair, and it looked like a rat's nest. I punked down on the couch and started fiddling with it, trying to finger comb the knots out. "You could say that. Izzy went out with some friends. I was going to stay home but I wound up going out. With a friend." Some friends? I hadn't mentioned Micha to him before. It seemed like a bad idea.

"Ah, good! I'm happy you are starting to reach out. Six months is a long time to be in a city without making connections."

Didn't I know it. I'd grown to love the atmosphere, the crazy layout, and the weird rules that made up Montreal, but it was fucking miserable having nowhere to go but home and work. I said as much, settling back onto the couch.

Dr. Archambault asked about Adam; how we'd met, the things we talked about.

I told him we talked about books, but I didn't know him very well—both of which were true. We had talked about books when we first met, but there hadn't been much time for get-to-know-you chatter when we'd been running for our lives.

I rubbed my arms. Even though Montreal summers are desperately hot and humid, I still wore long sleeves every day, just like I had for months. The scars were still too fresh. I didn't want to see them and I didn't want other people to see them. And now I didn't want anyone to see the spider bites or the deep scratches, either.

"Do you feel more comfortable, now that you are making friends?" he asked.

"I don't know," I said honestly. "I'm not used to being around people. It's weird. And I don't always know what to say. I never know what to say."

Out of habit, I reached into my bag and pulled out my

knitting project. Having something to do with my hands helped my mind focus and my body relax. "People are weird. Society is weirder. You're expected to do all of these things when you're around people, and I just don't understand it. That was the thing that got me back in Toronto. Everyone kept asking if I was okay, but if I told the truth then things always got awkward and I was complaining, but if I just said *I'm fine* then I was lying and being cold." Suddenly I didn't want to talk about it anymore. I knit a little faster.

Dr. A made a note on his pad and checked the clock. "Since we're a little short on time today, why don't we file this away for later, eh? Did you bring something to show me today?"

I nodded and put down my current project to retrieve the remaining contents of the tote. "This is the piece I was telling you about, the one I did with Dr. Fisher." I passed the woven material across the desk. About the size of a placemat, it was a weaving sample I'd done at St. Mary's. Dr. Fisher had seen my interest in crafts and textiles, and brought in a little tabletop loom. She was trying to teach me to make a scarf, but I ran out of time. Instead, I wound up with a tapestry about the size of a legal pad.

"Tell me about this," Archambault said, laying it out on top of his notes.

"At first I was just playing around with colors. I liked the yellows and the reds and the way they were blending, and the black was really soft. I kind of got bored just doing straight lines, so I started zig-zagging and doing different things, and then I added a couple more colors, and this is what came out."

"And what did Dr. Fisher have to say about the results?"

"It was kind of weird. Like, on the one hand she was really excited, but on the other she found it disturbing. I guess it's kind of understandable." I'd picked up the skill pretty quickly, but I guess shrinks wouldn't be doing their jobs if they didn't get concerned when the first thing that comes out is an image of flames and what looks like a shadowy person being burned. "The shadow there, that wasn't me, though. That's just the way the yarn pooled." It was a black, grey, and blue variegated yarn. Somehow, all the black portions had come together into a vague human shape. "I swear, it wasn't intentional."

"How do you feel about the result?"

"I don't like it. I decided weaving isn't for me. I'll stick to my needles," I said, picking my sock up again.

The doctor smiled. "No, I mean, how does the image make you feel?"

I looked down at my knitting. "I don't like that, either. I don't like fire. I've always been kind of afraid of it. I was trying to make something beautiful, and that came out instead." Story of my life. I try to do something good, and instead I wind up burning someone at the stake by accident.

Micha rested a hand on my shoulder and I twitched. He knew better than to interact with me in front of the head doctor; he pulled back quickly.

"It's kind of strange, though," I said, trying to distract myself. "I've seen this image before. I don't know where, but I've seen it. It shows up a lot in my dreams."

"Can you tell me about these dreams?"

I shook my head. "I usually don't remember them. I just remember fire when I wake up." I wasn't even looking at him anymore. I was just staring at my sock, knitting as fast as I could.

Archambault scribbled a few more notes, stroking his

chin thoughtfully. Then he reached into a drawer and came around the desk.

"I'd like to try something, if you're agreeable. These images have showed up in other work you did at St. Mary's, and I found references to them in your former doctor's notes. You've also mentioned them with me. I'd like to see if perhaps we can uncover their root through hypnosis."

I put down my work. "I don't know." Every time I saw them, I got scared.

Glancing up, I tried to catch Micha's eye. He appeared beside me. "You might not like what you see. But it might help you to understand."

Just full of useful information, that one. I don't know what I ever did without him.

"Okay. Let's do it." Pushing the yarn aside, I lay back on the couch. I was already having nightmares at least once or twice a week; going into another one couldn't be any worse, right? And hey, if it helped me sleep better, that would only be a win in the end, right?

I closed my eyes and let Dr. A do his thing. "Relax. Find a comfortable position. Feel your back, neck, and shoulders relaxing. All worries are minor and have no place here, now. Your breath is coming slowly, and you exhale any fears. Your muscles are relaxed, even down to your fingers and toes."

He waited a beat, then continued, "You're in a safe place. A familiar, safe room where nothing bad can reach you. Can you see the room?"

"Yes." It was the guest room at my uncle Mike's house. I used to stay there for a week every summer when I was a kid. I was ten years old again, with my rainbow suitcase open on the bed and the smell of popcorn drifting down the hall. Popcorn and ice cream were always dinner on movie nights.

"Good. Now go to the door, but don't open it yet. I want you to think of the fire, and why you fear it so much. When you open the door, you will see it, but know it can't hurt you. We are here only to observe. If you don't want to leave this room, then you don't have to.

"Now, I want you to open the door."

I did.

"What do you see?"

"The temple is on fire."

"Tell me about this temple."

"It's burning. They set it on fire," I said, squirming. I wanted to close the door. I didn't want to see. The flames licked at tall pillars; tapestries dissolved into ash, fire eating its way up intricate patterns.

Micha appeared next to me and slipped his hand into mine. "I'm right here. It can't hurt you. It's already over," he said. But when he turned back to the scene, his brows drew together.

"Where are we?" I asked. I knew the temple. I knew it, and I didn't know it. On the other side of the flames there was a statue of a woman with three heads. The paint on her marble features bubbled and smoked. Stone cracked from the heat.

More shadows were visible, darting in and out of darkness and smoke. Crashing, screaming—I'd been here before, but when?

Micha squeezed my hand. "There's only one way to find out."

We took that step together, crossing the threshold.

Up until that point, the images had been hazy and insubstantial. I was in my room at Uncle Mike's, but I was also aware it was only in my head. It was a memory of a place.

As soon as I went through the door, it was like getting sucked into a furnace.

I was no longer ten and in my favorite place with my favorite person. I was barefoot on a stone floor with the most intense heat I'd ever felt turning my bare arms red.

Coughing, I turned around. The door was gone. My only way out cut off, and I was left standing alone in the middle of the temple, the altar at my back.

I held a whip in my right hand, a thick braid of waxed rope with sharp copper beads at the end like arrowheads. When they came for me, I lashed out, slicing into exposed flesh.

The other initiates were long gone; dead, or taken as slaves. I couldn't see any of the priestesses, and assumed they had met the same fate.

I would not be a slave, not to any man. I gripped the handle of my weapon tight and struck again, copper tearing into the throat of my enemy and dropping him to the floor. I let the momentum carry me in a circle, bringing me around to another. With the whip raised over my head, I snapped the long rope in his direction. It wrapped around his neck and I pulled him to the ground.

But there was another and another. There were too many for me, and then one of my copper beads caught in my victim's helmet. He grabbed the rope and jerked it from my grasp. The coarse material tore at my skin as it went, drawing blood on my palms.

"Forgive me," I said, snatching a votive dish of oil from the altar. I threw it on him. He laughed—until I kicked him squarely in the chest, and he stumbled from the dais and into the fire.

I ran around the altar. Sparks had already left scorch marks on our most valued treasure. Too short to reach the rod, I gave a yank, ripping it from its mount. It tore, but I could fix it later. I had to get the tapestry out of the temple.

Someone grabbed me from behind, lifting me off my feet. I screamed and kicked, but it was no good.

Metal on metal. Then my attacker stiffened, a long scream erupting by my ear. I hit the ground and rolled out of the way as he collapsed, Micha's sword protruding from his side.

"Are you all right?" he asked, offering me a soot stained, bloody hand. I prayed none of it was his own.

I took it. "Yes. Thank you. Help me with this."

Together we managed to bundle the tapestry into a roll. I threw it over my shoulder, carrying it to the secret crypt entrance with Micha following behind, blade at the ready, cutting down anyone who tried to block our path.

Hidden behind another tapestry and accessed through a mechanism in one of the statues of Hekate Trivia, I led the way down into the catacombs. I took one of the torches from the wall and thrust the end into the fire. The tunnel swallowed us, and the door slammed shut.

We descended deep into the earth where the elder sisterhood of the temple were buried.

"Where are we going?" Micha asked, looking around nervously. He held the torch aloft, straining to make out landmarks in the dark.

"Down. There's a chamber where we can hide this, at least for now. It's too heavy to carry long distances. The tunnels come out near the river. We can come back for the tapestry later," I said.

"You should leave it. It's only a tapestry."

"It's a magic tapestry, a gift from the goddess herself. It shows the future. I can't let them have it."

The thick stone walls dampened the noise from above, but the sounds of the battle still carried through here and there. Our little village was no match for the invading force, particularly one ruthless enough to loot our only major temple.

"Is it true what they say about the caves?" Micha asked.

"That they lead directly to the underworld? I don't know." If they did, only the High Priestess knew, and she was dead now. If there *was* a gateway, I didn't want to find it on this particular excursion.

I shifted the tapestry to my other shoulder and kept walking, trying to ignore the tight, dark space. I'd been into the catacombs many times to perform my duties, but never without at least three other initiates and one of the priestesses.

"I won't get in trouble for being here, will I?" Micha asked, pausing to examine one of the mosaics on the wall.

I touched his wrist, just above his sword hand. "You are here in the service of Hekate, protecting her treasure and one of her servants. I doubt she will bring her wrath on you simply because you are not a woman."

He nodded, then leaned down to kiss me.

"What was that for?"

He shook his head. "Just in case."

I put my hand to his cheek. "The next full moon. We will survive, we will get out, and we will wed. Just as we planned."

A thump from somewhere behind us. I glanced over my shoulder, then moved as quickly as I could down the corridor.

From niches carved into the walls, the empty skulls of generations gone by watched our progress. Here and there we passed openings large enough to walk through, entrances to dedicated tombs of wealthy or important people.

"Ninth doorway, ninth column," I mumbled, counting. "Ninth row, ninth skull."

The ninth skull wasn't bone, but alabaster. Reaching into the empty eyes, I triggered the opening.

Initiates weren't supposed to know about the room, but I did. I'd been with some of the others, cleaning the resting places of our predecessors and leaving offerings, when I heard a noise. When I followed it, I saw our High Priestess opening the door.

It was the safest place I could think of under the circumstances. I left the tapestry on the floor and backed out, closing the door.

No sooner had it latched then a soldier rounded the corner, a wicked grin on his face.

"Evadne, run!" Micha ordered, stepping between him and me.

To my right was clear passage to the hidden exit by the river. But I couldn't leave Micha, not when two more men arrived.

The tight quarters made a battle with swords nearly impossible, particularly if that fight was three against one.

Micha raised his sword, jabbing the closest one in the side. His sword skimmed off armor, missing flesh by the width of a finger. His opponent brought his fists down on the back of his neck, sending Micha sprawling to the ground in a daze. Before he could roll out of the way, one of the other soldiers drove his spear into Micha's shoulder.

He howled in pain and I screamed, throwing myself over him. "Stop! Leave him alone!" I cried, torn between removing the weapon, and allowing him to bleed with nothing to stop it.

The soldiers laughed, and the one with the spear

retrieved his spear, yanking it roughly from Micha's body. He choked on another scream. I tore off my shawl to press it to his wound, but one of the other men grabbed my arms and hauled me to my feet.

"This one is coming with us," he said, holding my chin in his meaty hands and turning my head side to side. "Not the prettiest, but she'll do!" They roared with laughter again.

Micha managed to get himself into a kneeling position. Still holding his sword, he raised it—

And then one of the soldiers struck, his own blade slicing Micha's head from his body so quickly I didn't even have time to scream.

I couldn't move. Frozen, I stared at his body as it listed to one side before collapsing.

"No!" The one holding me tightened his grip, pulling me away from Micha. I screamed and struggled, punching, kicking, biting, anything I could do to cause them harm. He merely crushed me into his arms until I couldn't breathe, until one of his friends managed to tie my hands.

I was so busy with my useless struggle, I didn't even notice the smoke until one of them swore.

"This way!" he said, leading them deeper into the catacombs.

"No. You can't go that way! There's no exit."

"What do you mean, there's no exit?" my captor demanded, shaking me so hard spots appeared in front of my eyes.

"It caved in, ages ago. That way is a dead end. The only way out is back through the temple," I lied. "If you try to get out that way, you'll be trapped and the smoke will kill you."

"Ha, so you think we should try our luck with the

flames?" Micha's killer asked.

"The temple is made of stone. Once the contents burn, the building itself should be safe. You have a chance to get out. Unless you'd rather say down here and wait for the smoke to fill the tunnels, then suffocate."

The three of them exchanged looks. After a brief debate, we turned around, running for the narrow stairs. The one I took to be the leader, who was also the tallest, led the way with the torch, head bent against the low ceilings of the crypt. Micha's murderer followed; I glared at his back with enough hatred and anger to make Ares happy for decades. He, too, had to duck, though not so much as his friend.

Still bound, they dragged me along like an insubordinate dog behind the broadest of the trio. If my throat had not already been dry from screaming and smoke, I would have spit on him.

I wiped my eyes, the scene replaying in my mind as we ran. It had all happened so quickly I couldn't do anything to stop it. One moment, I'd been holding Micha's hand, and the next he was gone.

The temple had been decimated in our absence; the tapestries reduced to ash, the bodies of my sisters provided additional fuel for hungry flames. The air was thick with the smell of burning flesh. Smoke filled my lungs at the first breath.

"This way!" One of them said, leading us off to the right, past the ruined altar.

Feigning a coughing fit, I bent double. My captor pulled at my ropes, dragging me after him. I stumbled, hands brushing the ground. I came up with the sword of his fallen comrade.

Surprise was the only reason I managed to drive the blade into him at all. It pierced through the lacing at the side of his armor, and I used all my weight to force it deeper into his chest.

Blood spilled from his mouth as I released the handle. He stumbled backward off the dais, eyes as lifeless as the empty marble gaze of Hekate's statue.

I turned mine on the two remaining men. "You lack the honor to be called soldiers. To desecrate a temple, to kill the women and children who serve it for no other reason than to feed your own greed brings shame upon you, and the gods will take their revenge. But not before I take mine. This is my home. My family. And that," I pointed at the tunnel door we had just exited, "was my betrothed. In the name of the Shadow Goddess, I curse you. May your feet ever wander, finding no rest. May you be as homeless as the innocent people you have deposed. May the shadows grow around you until they consume you, making your path so dark even Hades will not find your souls!"

The one who had killed Micha appeared somewhat disturbed by my declaration, particularly when a section of ceiling collapsed directly behind him, showering him with sparks. I watched with satisfaction as dozens of tiny burns appeared on his arms and legs.

The other seemed more anxious to get out alive than with any dignity. "Worthless wench!" Kicking out, he sent me tumbling back, into the unintended pyre of my sisterhood.

I jolted awake before Dr. A could give the signal. Heart hammering, I gulped in clean air.

Micha sat beside me, his hand gripping mine like a vise.

Dr. Archambault was also kneeling on the floor, his eyes so wide with worry that the brows were in their proper place for the first time since I'd met him.

"Are you all right? I have never had a patient have such a violent reaction to hypnosis before!"

"I—I'm fine." I was shaking all over, crying. It had all felt so real, every second of it.

The doctor was saying something, but I wasn't listening. I needed to get out of there, away from the tomb-like office.

"Could you perhaps have read it somewhere? Or seen it in a movie? Some would argue the past life theory, of course, but I don't think—"

"I'm sorry, I need to go," I said, grabbing my bag and running for the door.

Somehow, I got lucky and did not have a parking ticket for once. The Jeep roared to life with minimal persuasion, and I pulled out into traffic as fast as I could.

Right then, I wished for one of those long, winding country roads people go on about, but I'm a city girl—born and bred—so Montreal streets it was. But I followed them to one of the few places in the city where I stood a shot at being alone.

# Chapter Four
## Unraveling

The Chalet resembles a giant stone hunting lodge from the outside, since at one point, that's what it was. Two stories high, the interior is all open and mostly empty, the tourist attractions having mostly vacated in favor of more popular areas of Mount Royal—except for a souvenir shop the size of a closet.

The building boasted a massive stone terrace with a breathtaking view of the city center. I claimed a spot at the railing, staring out at downtown without seeing it. My head still spun with images from my dream. Vision? Memory? What was it?

Micha stood behind me. Hesitantly, he placed a hand on my shoulder. Sensing I wouldn't pull away, he wrapped his arms around me. I needed a hug after that. It didn't matter if it came from a ghost or my worst enemy or my mom; I just needed the contact.

"What was that?" There was no one around but I still whispered, afraid of speaking too loudly.

"I don't know."

"You were there."

"I know. I saw it. But I don't remember it."

"How can you not remember it?"

"You don't remember it, either."

"That's different. You're a ghost or something, shouldn't you—"

"No. I'm a spirit. I've never been alive, Evie, that's what I tried to tell you. That wasn't me. It *couldn't* have been."

But there was doubt in his voice.

I laced my fingers through his. "But that was me, wasn't it? That girl—Evadne. She was me. I'm her. I felt it."

Micha rested his cheek against the top of my head. "I think so. Maybe an incarnation before I arrived. It would have to be a long time ago; she was talking about Greek gods." His voice trailed off into thoughtful silence. "But it would explain a lot. About you. About what you can do."

"How?"

A father and his young daughter wandered across the flagstones, the little girl laughing and skipping, holding an ice cream cone in one hand. Her father put a quarter into the magnifiers, and hoisted her up so she could see the city below.

"Not here," Micha said, pulling away.

***

Mount Royal is crisscrossed with an enormous network of trails. Some are paved; some are barely a track through the woods. I followed one of these lesser-known paths to a quiet spot high on the mountain but lacking the view.

Surrounded by dense forest, the circle of three boulders the size of Smart cars had been my thinking place since I'd come to Montreal. I discovered it by accident one day while I was out walking, and now it was my favorite spot when I needed to get away from people but also didn't want to be at home.

A steep, three meter drop on one side, a narrow, almost invisible trail, no view to speak of, and only enough room for one or two people to sit comfortably meant it was not a place easily stumbled upon by accident.

I slid down one of the boulders into the soft, mossy hollow between them. Traffic was barely audible, the voices of the people in the park nearly nonexistent, except for the rare outdoorsman who chose to walk directly below. The radio towers above meant cell reception was almost nil, thanks to interference.

I pulled out my knitting and forced myself to take several deep breaths. Micha sat quietly beside me, watching me work, waiting until my hands found the right rhythm before he told me his story.

"Every human soul has at least a couple of others attached to it from the time it takes up residence in a newborn child: guides, guardians. Sometimes the souls of loved ones take up those roles, but more often than not it's spirits.

"While a human child might one day become a ghost, a spirit is something different entirely. We've never been, and never will be, alive. We're not compatible with human bodies. We just kind of ride along, providing a sixth sense. Warnings against danger, that kind of thing.

"I don't remember the first time I saw your soul. At least, not clearly. Only that there was nothing, and then there was light. And when I followed it, it led me to you. Or rather, one of your former incarnations.

"I stayed with her for eighteen years, through war,

plague, and famine. I watched your—her—family crumble from nobility to slaves over the course of a week, until she was killed by her new master. She was an innocent bystander in someone else's war. She was in the wrong place at the wrong time, and I couldn't warn her to get away.

"Eugeneia didn't deserve that. She brought her father meals every day at the library. They used their wealth to help the less fortunate in Alexandria. It was just the two of them. All they wanted to do was read and learn and protect the knowledge they had for the future, but instead they were murdered."

I almost dropped my needles. "Wait…are you saying that in a past life, I was at the library of Alexandria?"

Micha nodded. "Your father was a scholar. Women weren't technically allowed in, but you would bring him his lunch every day, and no one bothered you if you read a scroll or two while you were there.

"Maybe it was guilt, but I couldn't just move on to another charge after that. I knew there must have been something I could do to prevent her death, so I waited. I stayed with her as she waited to be reincarnated, and then chose to stay with her through her next lifetime. When that one ended badly, too, I thought it was my fault. I felt like I owed it to her to set things right, so I continued to stay, watching over that same soul as it was reincarnated over and over again, in various parts of the world in different forms. But no matter what I did or didn't do, she always met with an unlucky, untimely end.

"The third time it happened, I realized something must be wrong. By the fourth, things got really messy. Accusations of witchcraft ended in a trial and a burning, and it only got worse from there. Murder, abuse, torture. I couldn't stop it. I couldn't protect her. No matter what I did, I was bound to watch her—you—suffer in silence, always alone.

"And every time you've been reincarnated, you've gotten a little weaker. A little less able to fight. Italy. England. The New World. The Old West. No matter where or when, it's always the same.

"Then, last time…"

When I looked up at him, he wouldn't look at me, his face full of pain.

Staring at a point in the distance, he continued slowly: "Your name was Jenny, then. It was the 1930s, and not a great time to be much of anywhere, but a little farming community in the middle of the Dust Bowl? That was probably the worst.

"Your—Jenny's—family was horrible. Youngest of twelve, she grew up being abused in every way possible by brothers, cousins, and her parents. If her mother thought she was bad, she'd lock her in a closet, sometimes for days on end, with no food.

"When she was sixteen, she met and married a man who promised to take care of her, but he was just as bad as what she was running from, if not worse."

I couldn't remember any of this, but the more I listened the more it sounded like a story I might have heard when I was a kid, but none of the details sounded familiar. When Micha continued, his voice was so low I almost couldn't hear it. "When…when Jenny found out that she was pregnant, she knew that bringing a child into that house would be the worst possible thing that she could do." He looked at me with tears in his eyes. "I wanted to convince her to run, but she had no place to go and no way to get there. The things that her brothers had done to her as a child left her disabled; she wouldn't be able to work even if she could find a job. There weren't a lot of resources back then for battered women, and none of them were nearby. Her nearest neighbors were miles away, and as far as they knew her husband was a pillar of the community, one who was always looking out for others. Especially young girls."

"But he was preying on them." It wasn't hard to fill in the blank.

Micha nodded. "She found out only a few weeks after discovering the baby. She hadn't told her husband. She came downstairs in the middle of the night to find another girl, in the same situation, begging him for help. He denied everything, and when she still wouldn't leave, he threatened her."

"Jenny waited until he went back to bed. He drank himself stupid all the time, so she waited until one night when he was passed out. Then she slipped out of bed, and did the only thing that she felt was left."

"She killed him." I closed my eyes, clutching my needles tightly, though by now they lay still in my lap.

"She got a can of kerosene from the kitchen and poured it on the bed, and lit it on fire."

I sucked in a breath, but he wasn't done.

"Jenny couldn't run. She could barely walk most days. She had no place to go and knew she would never make it to one of the neighbors on her own. She also knew what she was doing was murder. Over the years, she'd heaped all the blame for everything onto herself. So when she lit the match, she didn't run. She went to the closet and shut the door."

I didn't know what to think or how to respond. I watched Micha wipe his eyes, with my mouth open, knitting forgotten in my lap.

I couldn't remember any of it, but I felt like I'd failed him somehow. And then to make him go through it again… "I'm so sorry."

"No. Don't apologize. Not to me. You never need to apologize to me." His voice was forceful. "Jenny did what she thought was best, and as often as I've gone over things since then, I don't know what she could have done differently. She lived in almost complete isolation; there was no one she could have gone to for help, and she wasn't physically capable of getting out or defending herself on her own. I even…I tried to find someone to help her, but there was no one within my range."

"What is your range?" I asked, suddenly curious.

He shrugged. "It varies. Sometimes it's only a few meters. Sometimes I can go up to a kilometer." With his knees drawn up to his chest, he stared at his hands. "I held her hand at the end. I always did that. But I think you might have seen me that time."

I reached for his hand now. "I don't know. I don't remember. But I'm glad I can see you now."

He gave my fingers a squeeze. I wondered if he'd ever told anyone this story before. Did spirits have a union? Did he have friends? Chats with the ghost from down the street? Or was he alone, doomed to follow me around for the rest of my life? For eternity?

"I'm not doomed," he mumbled. "I like being with you. If I didn't, then I wouldn't keep trying to save your sorry ass." His lips twitched up into a half-hearted attempt at a smile. "I chose to be with you. And I will continue to choose to be with you, no matter what. It doesn't matter if you can see me or not, or if you don't believe me or think you're crazy. I'm right where I want to be."

"Masochist." But I smiled and scooted over to sit beside him.

"Yeah, well, it's an occupational hazard."

I laid my head on his shoulder. "So how is it I can see you now? I mean, that's what, eight lives lived when I had no idea you existed, and now all of a sudden you're here?"

Micha ran his thumb absently over the back of my hand. He was still cold all over, but I found that I'd gotten used to it. In fact, in a muggy Montreal summer with temperatures around thirty degrees celsius, it was like having my own personal air conditioner. "When a person dies violently, it damages their soul. Bruises it, if you will. Eventually those bruises will heal, but they might leave a scar or a mark of some kind behind. A particular behavior or a way of thinking that is a result of the trauma. When they take their own life, however, the damage is much more severe. It fractures it. One fracture, it might be able to heal from over a few centuries, but two? Those are cracks that won't heal again. It's less like a broken bone and more like a mirror. Once the glass is broken, you can't repair it, you can only replace it. But I think that those cracks are the reason you can see me. Your mirror might be cracked, but it isn't broken yet."

"So what happens when it breaks?"

"Once those pieces begin to flake off, the soul falls apart. It gets recycled. It's no longer a specific soul, but is cosmic compost to make new souls."

"So if I had…if I'd managed to do it…."

"No more Evie. No more you." He reached up to brush a lock of hair from my face. "No more second chances."

"And you?"

"I don't know. I might be forced to take a new charge."

"Or the same thing could happen to you."

"Very possible."

"So maybe it's a good thing. That I lived." It was the first time since St. Mary's I'd considered the possibility.

Micha tugged my sleeve up with one hand, revealing the long scar on my wrist. It wasn't red anymore, but it was still raised and ugly, new looking. He put a hand over it. "Maybe. But if walking away now and never seeing you again meant you could be whole, I would do it."

# Chapter Five
# Talking to the Walls

I was full of nervous energy when I got home. Still processing what I'd seen in the vision, I wanted to research and find out more about what I'd seen, but when I sat down at my laptop I couldn't focus. After a lot of internal debate, I changed into yoga pants, sneakers, and a T-shirt and went out for a run.

I'm not usually big on the whole physical activity thing, but sometimes there's just no substitute for getting hot and sweaty. If anyone had been watching me, they probably would have laughed at the skinny girl with no muscles, so pale she could be used as a caution sign for nighttime road work, running through the streets of Montreal in a baggy men's shirt emblazoned with an evil smiley face. I was so out of shape that for every block I managed to jog, I had to walk for two.

*It's not about what other people think.* One of the things I was supposed to be doing per my instructions from Dr. Fisher was work out more. Endorphins. Healthy lifestyle and all of that. I'd even gone out and bought running shoes once I was released from St. Mary's, but never got around to using them. I was more of a stay-at-home-and-read-a-book-or-knit kind of girl, rather than the go-out-running-and-take-yoga kind of girl.

Since I'd just come from the mountain, I decided to head north. Outremont has some of the prettiest parks in the city, and the one named for the neighborhood is probably the most beautiful. With sculpted earth- and stoneworks, water features, and a charming little bridge, it's a great place to hang out with a book. Or yarn. Or a cute guy.

I brushed that last thought away quickly. I don't know what happened to my head. Somehow, I'd gone from crazy to drooling in sixty seconds flat when it came to Micha. It just felt very natural to be with him. He put me at ease. I wasn't scared when I was with him. I didn't feel like he was passing judgement every time I opened my mouth. Or when I didn't. That was a rare thing for me. It was so much easier to curl up inside my shell where no one could reach, but he gave me a reason to venture out.

Normally, I wasn't the type to even notice guys. Sure, I might occasionally find one that was cute, but the appeal usually went away as soon as they opened their mouths. I was the only girl I knew whose parents were trying to set her up with *anyone*, instead of cleaning the shotgun every time her date showed up. Mom said it was because they wanted me to be happy. I was pretty sure it was just because they wanted me to be at least semi-normal.

Blushing, I slowed my pace as I entered the park. It was weird to be thinking about Micha when I knew he could hear everything in my head—which really wasn't fair. Who decided this whole telepathy thing was one-way, anyhow? Why couldn't I read Micha's mind? Turnabout was fair play, after all.

Since it was the middle of a weekday, most people

were still at work, and except for an old woman with a
book wearing a funny little hat with a veil in the far
corner of the park, it was deserted. I jogged a circuit
around the pond at the center of the park, and came up by
the memorial wall, a marker for Montreal soldiers killed
in World Wars One and Two. On the east side, there was
statue of an angel covering her face and weeping. Very
*Doctor Who*.

I can't say why, but that statue resonated with me
somehow. I didn't know a single name on the list, but the
distraught angel was a fabulous, emotional piece of art,
and it was impossible to walk past her without feeling
something.

Panting, I plopped down on a bench, leaning forward
to catch my breath. When I sat upright again, I jumped. A
uniformed man was sitting beside me, and I was sure he
hadn't been there a second earlier.

"I'm sorry, I didn't mean to scare you," he said in
French.

"No, it's okay," I gasped, my heart still tapping out an
aggressive rhythm against my ribs. I stuttered over the
words as my brain struggled to switch languages. "You
just startled me."

"I hate to ask, but do you know where Anna is? Anna
Dugray. She's tall and blond and has green eyes. I've been
waiting for so long, she should be here by now. You
haven't seen her, have you?"

I shook my head. It was a little weird talking to a
stranger, but I'd seen him around before. I figured he
lived in the area.

"Do you have her number? Maybe you should call
her," I suggested, getting up to try some stretches. I could
already feel my calves threatening to seize up on me.

"I can't," he said sadly.

On a whim, I pulled my cell phone from my pocket. My hand partially outstretched to offer it to him, I realized something.

I'd seen him before. I remembered his uniform. It was military, Army, I thought, but looked nothing like the uniforms I was used to seeing.

Because the uniform was seventy years out of date.

"I…I need to go," I said quickly.

"Oh. Well, thank you anyway. If you see her, will you tell her Etienne is looking for her?"

"Yeah. Sure." I turned and ran like the owls from hell were chasing me all over again. I nearly got run over by a Fiat as a I crossed the street.

*That was a ghost. A ghost! Right there! In broad daylight!*

Micha scoffed. "Hardly the strangest thing you've seen lately. And it's not like he's the first ghost you've seen."

"What the hell are you talking about?" I wheezed, pausing at a red light.

Micha appeared beside me, leaning on the traffic light pole. "Do you remember the two nuns you passed on your way to Dr. Archambault's this morning? Or the guy in the suit who was waiting in his office? What about those women in the long dresses outside of the church on Mount Royal Avenue?"

"You have got to be kidding me."

Micha shook his head. "I didn't say anything because I didn't want to freak you out. I thought it would be better if you realized it on your own. But you've been seeing ghosts and spirits on and off ever since you woke up."

I could have strangled him. "And you're just telling me this now because…?"

He rolled his eyes. "Because you can be a little dense

sometimes. I mean, did you really think there was a convention in town or something?"

"It's Montreal. There's always a festival or a convention in town. This city gave birth to Cirque du Solei; weirdos are kind of par for the course."

"And all of the historical costumes…?"

I shrugged defensively. "I figured it was some kind of historical reenactment group."

Micha chuckled. "See, this is why you need me to keep an eye on you. You can be impossibly short sighted."

"Shut up. I'm only just getting used to the fact that you're not a hallucination and I'm not crazy."

As soon as I said it, an older lady and her tiny dog walked past. She took one look at me, panting, sweating, and talking to a light post, picked up her dog, and hurried off in the other direction.

"Great. Stop laughing. It's not funny."

"That depends on which side of reality you're on."

I stuck my tongue out at him and jogged across Côte-Sainte-Catherine. Instead of following, he merely popped up on the other side of the street with a grin on his face.

"Okay, that's cheating," I gasped, pausing to catch my breath. "You just get to teleport around, and I'm over here doing all of the actual work."

"Consider it motivation," he replied, grin still firmly in place.

"If you count the urge to punch you right now motivation."

"Hey now, play nice. Is this how you repay me for trying to get you into shape?"

"No. It's revenge for you being a smug bastard."

His eyes twinkled as he fell into step beside me. I wasn't really mad. Barely even annoyed.

My hand brushed his as we walked. I linked my fingers through his, recalling the dream once again. The ghost of the soldier had distracted me for a while, but I needed to sort through the things I'd seen.

"Do you think it was real?" I asked.

Micha only shrugged. "I don't know. I know it came from your memories—deep memories, the kind you can't normally get to on your own. But I don't know how it could be possible. I'm not human. I never was." He paused.

A thought tickled the back of my brain—

"No. Don't go there," he said firmly.

"What?"

"You thought… You were wondering about what you saw. The other version of us. But it's not real. It can never happen, Evie. Even if it was possible for a spirit to be reincarnated, you're talking about bringing someone back from the dead, not rebirth. They're two completely different things."

"But—"

"No." He dropped his hand, staring at his fingers for a moment. "I wasn't joking when I said I would walk away from you for good if it meant you could be whole again. Don't go falling in love with me, just because of some stupid dream.

"Falling for me would be easy. You know I won't leave you. You know how much I care about you. You know that no matter your faults, I will always be here. It wouldn't require you to change, to seek other people. But you have to. You can't just wrap yourself up in the familiar and the safe for the rest of your life. You need someone who can actually be there for you. Someone *real*."

At some point in his soliloquy, we'd stopped. I turned

and started walking again, faster than before. "I don't know what you're so worried about," I said quickly. "I'm not falling for you. That would be ridiculous. And kind of sad." Really. Falling in love with a ghost? Or a spirit, or whatever? No matter what you called him, he existed primarily in my head.

My shrinks would have a field day with that.

I suddenly wondered at the wisdom of not telling Dr. A or any of the docs back in Toronto about Micha.

I looked back over my shoulder. Micha looked even more uncomfortable than I felt, and he had the same kicked puppy look he'd had that morning on the Mountain.

I still had questions for him. And, I realized belatedly, I needed to call Adam.

Izzy was supposed to be working at home all afternoon, which meant whispered conversations in the bedroom about things that weren't supposed to exist or even be remotely possible.

Yeah, this wouldn't be awkward at all.

***

Izzy was in the zone when I got home, typing away madly on her laptop, so I left her to work in peace and slipped back to my bedroom. I put on some music as camouflage, and then fished out the scrap of paper with Adam's number on it. The last thing I wanted was for my guardian to overhear a conversation about ghosts and graveyards and rabid owls when I was supposed to be under psychiatric care. Izzy was pretty laid back, but I doubted even she would take that very well.

The phone rang five times, then went to voicemail. After the standard "leave a message after the beep," I said, "Hey. It's me. Evie. Um, the girl from the bookshop? Er, the graveyard? Anyway, I wanted to know if you were okay. I mean, I know you were kind of shaken up and I don't blame you because that was pretty weird, but um, call me back. If you want. I totally understand if you don't. Want to, that is. God, this is really awkward. So um, I'll just go, and you can call me, my number is—" The beep that meant I was a rambling loser cut me off, and offered other options, like hanging up now. I decided it was the best one.

I hung up and tossed the phone on bed, flopping down beside it. Micha appeared, leaning against the footboard. "You still have some explaining to do, you know," I said. "What the hell happened last night? What was that light? And what was up with those owls? And why could Adam see you? And what the heck is going on?"

My ringtone cut him off. Adam's number was on the screen.

"Hello?"

"I…Hi?"

"It's um, it's Adam."

"Yeah."

"I just ah…I wanted to return your call. So, I'm okay."

"You don't sound okay." He sounded like he hadn't slept, and like he was jumping at shadows.

"I'm fine. Just kind of tired."

Micha started gesturing at me.

"Hang on a second." I covered the mouthpiece.

"Have him meet you. Tonight, at the cemetery."

"Why?"

"Because I don't like to repeat myself and it'll be better if you're both there. Besides, if he only sees me once, he can brush it off. If he sees me twice, then I'm real. At least to him."

"Yeah, but why the cemetery? Why not here? Or a café? Or that nice Chinese place that just opened up?"

Micha gave me a look like that was the dumbest question he'd heard all day. "Because the cemetery is where I'll have the best chance of making myself visible to people who aren't you."

I was about to object, but he waved me off.

"I'll explain it later."

I sighed. "Fine. Adam, are you still there?" I passed on Micha's message. Adam hesitated, but finally he agreed to meet me just after sunset, right where we'd met the dog last time. "Great. I will see you then."

Hanging up, I checked the clock. It was barely one in the afternoon, leaving me with about eight hours to kill.

I tiptoed to the living room, trying not to disturb my aunt. She had an office set up in a little nook at the other end of the flat, but preferred to do her work in the living room. Since she seldom entertained and her style of writing involved scattering Post-its, notecards, outlines, and reference materials all over the floor until the Ikea rug vanished under a sea of fifty percent post-consumer recycled goods, the preference was understandable even if her methods were not. Her entire "office" was roughly the size of the coffee table.

With an old episode of *Buffy* muted on the television, the hum of the DVD player and the manic tapping of her keyboard were the only sounds in the room. Color-coded notes littered the floor, along with evidence of her breakfast—a plate with bagel crumbs and smear of cream cheese on the edge—and lunch—a bag of microwave popcorn and a mint Aero bar. Nearby, her ashtray threatened to overflow, the afternoon's latest cigarette smoldering as it dangled from her lips. She hunched over the Mac on the ottoman, straddling the seat of her favorite chair. It was ergonomic, organic, and comfy as hell. It was also ugly as sin, clashed with everything else in the apartment, and cost more than I made in a year. Granted, I was putting in fifteen hours a week at minimum wage, but still.

Izzy was my dad's youngest sibling. Uncle Mike was two years older. Both of them had been "oops!" babies, born well after my grandparents thought they were done having kids. My dad was fourteen at the time, and Anne and Mary, my other aunts, were eleven and twelve.

The age difference created a pretty big rift between them, especially Izzy and the rest of the family. It doesn't help that she has the only wild streak in our conservative Italian family. She ran away from home when she was seventeen, putting five hundred kilometers and a language barrier between her and the rest of the Cappelli clan. My parents didn't like the idea of me coming to stay with her, but they had no clue what to do with me. All we did was fight. Uncle Mike was the one who finally convinced them. Dad hated the idea. Mom wasn't crazy about it, either, but decided it was better to send me to a wayward aunt than to send me back to the psych ward.

For starters, they didn't have to pay Izzy.

I suspected they still did, to help cover my living expenses, but I couldn't prove it.

Izzy had no idea how to handle me and my moods, either, but at least she tried, instead of yelling at me all the time. Another suspicion I had was she'd gone through the mental health thing herself after she moved out, though I doubt there had been padded rooms involved in her case. Just a lot of long hours of therapy, which eventually translated into a lot of novels. She wasn't *New*

*York Times* famous, but she'd won several genre awards and she had fans. Tumblr could be a pretty scary and fascinating place if you searched for her name, but Google was worse.

I examined her bookshelf as unobtrusively as possible. It was a mix of fantasy, science fiction, historical and contemporary mysteries, bodice rippers, and nonfiction covering everything from trains of the 1800s to modern witchcraft to a medical textbook from 1995 she'd gotten at a used bookstore for a dollar.

"I've got the ARC of Rose's new book on my desk if you want to read it," she said without looking up or pausing in her typing.

"Cool." An ARC was a sort of preview copy of a book sent out by publishers before the release. About half the books on Izzy's shelf were ARCs of her books, or books her other author friends had written.

"Have you finished reading those chapters?" Izzy asked, finally pausing long enough to crack her knuckles and look at me over the rims of her glasses.

"Most of them." I picked my way through the detritus of the writer at work, carefully plucking the sheaf of papers from the coffee table, where I'd left it the night before. "I'm done with the first three. I'll get the others tonight."

"What do you think so far?"

"I'm really liking it. I think Henry's voice might be a little too modern, though. And I wasn't sure about some of the geography as you explained it. I made a note at that section. And Morgan is hilarious. I love some of her quips."

Izzy smiled. "I thought you'd like those. You don't think the puns are overdone?"

I grinned. "I thought they were great, but you know

I'm not a fan of high-brow comedy. You haven't gone into Piers Anthony territory, though, so I think you've still got some room to play around with it."

"Good." She studied me for a minute. "Did something happen?"

"What do you mean?"

"Nothing. Just that it's good to see you smiling. You haven't really done that since you got here."

I looked away, uncomfortable.

She held out a hand to me. "Come here for a second."

I found a clear space by her chair and crouched there.

She smoothed my hair back from my face. "You're gorgeous, you know? No matter what anyone else tells you, no matter what that voice in your head says, you are beautiful and smart and perfect." She leaned over to give me a hug.

I hugged back, a little awkwardly. We're not really huggers, my family. My mom and I used to be, but no one else really is. And I had no idea where Izzy's little pep talk was coming from.

"I've got something special planned for your birthday. I hope you like it."

I'd completely forgotten about my birthday. Probably because I'd been feeling about as celebratory as a wet blanket. But there were only two more days to go until I turned eighteen.

"What do you want to do for your birthday, huh?" she asked, pulling back. "We could go see a movie, or go out to eat. Or I could see if there are any shows in town! There's always shows—ballet, or theater, or maybe a concert. You used to love going to theater when you were a kid. Remember when Mike and I took you to see the Nutcracker for Christmas?"

That was the year my dad got my mom a trip to

Hawaii for Christmas. Mom had gotten us all tickets to see the show, but it fell on the day they were supposed to leave. Instead of letting the tickets go to waste, Mom asked around and Mike volunteered to take me. Since Izzy was already in town for the Holidays, she came, too. It had been a fabulous show, the first time I got to do anything with Izzy without the watchful eyes of my parents and grandparents stalking our every move, waiting for my infamous aunt to corrupt her poor, innocent niece.

"Sounds like fun, but maybe we can just order in. Watch a movie or something. Low-key."

"Low-key, huh? Not going to go out and party, celebrate being an adult?"

I snorted. "Woe to anyone who confuses me with a responsible adult."

"Honey, if responsible was a requirement for adulthood, do you think I'd be where I am?" she asked, pulling me into another one-armed hug. "Okay, so pizza and a movie it is. Oh, and if we get any packages between now and then? Don't open them." She wiggled her eyebrows as she slid her glasses back on. That was my cue to get out of her way.

"Sure thing," I replied. I found the book I was looking for on the shelf, then grabbed the ARC on my way back to my room. I had a lot of reading to do.

***

By the time I was done with the last two chapters Izzy asked me to read, I'd finished knitting a sock. It might make me a knitting heathen, but I never block my socks, I just wear them. I popped them into my drawer, since late June in Montreal is way too warm to be wearing hand knit socks, anyway.

Finally, the sun began to sink in the sky. At some point, the television got unmuted, and I heard Izzy listening to the news. She flipped back and forth between the CBC and a local Montreal station, getting the information in English and French.

"I'm going out for a walk," I said, poking my head back into the living room. Her notes and books had been swept back up into piles surrounding her chair, the laptop closed on the footrest.

Izzy sounded doubtful. "Really? It's getting kind of late. It'll be dark soon."

"I won't be long. I thought it might be cool to catch a sunset from up on the mountain."

"That sounds nice. Do you want some company?" She started to get up. I started to object. We both froze, afraid of overstepping and offending the other.

"Maybe another time," Izzy said. She sounded a little disappointed.

"Yeah. Maybe for my birthday," I suggested. "I won't be long. Promise." *I hope*.

Izzy nodded. "Don't forget your phone."

I patted my pocket. It was weird when Izzy went into mom mode. She wasn't nearly as practiced at it as my actual mom, and it mostly just came out awkward.

I took the steps to the street two at a time. Once I reached the sidewalk, I kept looking upward for more owls or other homicidal avian maniacs.

When I looked down again, I swore.

After my jog, I'd had to scour my room for something to wear. It was laundry day, which meant I was stuck with a tank top in my usual black. I covered my arms with a pair of wrist warmers, but I still felt naked with three quarters of my arms showing, so I added a superfine lace poncho over top. It was just enough to cover my abused skin, which showed signs of not just the spider bites and my run-in with the crazy owls, but now appeared to have a pretty nasty sunburn as well, thanks to my workout.

What I hadn't noticed was the giant snag running down the front of my poncho. About a finger's length of thread dangled from the machine-knit fabric, causing an enormous pucker.

"Shit, now what?" I muttered, tugging at the surrounding area in a fruitless attempt to pull the thread back into place. "Go back, go back…."

I smoothed my hand over the area, wishing I could make the imperfection vanish.

And then, it did.

Before my eyes, the snag wriggled itself back into place, the pineapple lace pattern flattening out until it looked like new, the snapped fibers rejoining in the process.

*What the hell?*

"Evie!"

I looked up. Adam was across the street, waiting for me at the cemetery gate. He waved.

I waved back. Checking the street, I jogged over to him. "Hey."

"Hi."

"So I just got off of work. I brought some food." He held up a plastic bag with the logo for the corner store on it. Inside, a couple of bottles clanked. I caught up to him at the entrance we followed the path up to a bench encircling a tree. The night was warm, most of the humidity of the day having burned off already.

"So what's this about? Why meet here?" Adam asked, pulling two microwave burritos from the bag. He handed me one, along with a soda. The soda was still cold, the dep keeping its beverages at near freezing most of the time, while the burrito was lukewarm, having cooled on the walk over.

"It was my idea," Micha said, appearing on Adam's other side. "I thought this was the best place. I'm a little stronger here."

Adam jumped, nearly ending up in my lap. A glob of refried beans landed on his jeans, but he didn't take any notice. "Do not sneak up on me like that!" he said, brandishing the burrito in Micha's face and spraying him with rice.

"I'm a spirit. I can't *not* sneak," he said, brushing non-existent grains of rice from his shirt.

I decided I'd better intercede before things got out of hand. "So what exactly did you want to tell us that couldn't be said someplace less creepy?" I asked.

Micha stood, turning his attention back to me. "I wanted to test a theory. See—" He looked over at Adam. "Let me start at the beginning. No, there is too much. I will sum up."

I rolled my eyes.

He gave Adam a brief rundown on the difference between spirits and ghosts, and how he was most decidedly not the latter. Then he explained about staying with me for a whole bunch of different reincarnations, but skipped the part about why so many lifetimes had been involved.

"Every region has a link to the underworld. A place where it's easier to pass through one plane to the next. These are usually historically significant places, locations that hold a lot of energy for a region, both positive and negative.

"Mount Royal has one of those gateways. It's been an

epicenter of power since before white settlers reached
Canada. The dog you saw last night is commonly called a
Grim; they show up a lot in different forms in various
mythologies, but at its root, the Grim belongs to the ruler
of the Underworld."

"Wait, I read *Harry Potter*. This means we're going to
die, doesn't it? I mean, we saw the Grim—" Adam's voice
took on the same pitch Ron Weasly's did when he
mentioned the black dog of the underworld.

Micha waved him off. "No. You only die when you
see the Grim if his master tells him to attack. Or mistress,
in this case."

"Wait, what mythology are we talking about here?" I
asked. "Last night you said it was Hekate's dog, but she
doesn't rule the underworld."

"She didn't used to," Micha corrected. "See, for the
gods, power is everything. And their power comes from
belief. No one has really given the old gods much thought
for centuries, but the occult movement and the rise of
Wicca and other pagan religions in the last century or so
have started to bring them back. They're still barely a blip
on the cosmic radar, but thanks to all of the new and
regenerated religions popping up, Hekate is now one of
the most popular goddesses. More people believe and
worship her than they do in Hades. Ergo, the Underworld
has a new queen, and that means the Grim has a mistress,
not a master."

"What does this have to do with anything?" Adam
asked. He was still sitting rigidly beside me, his back
pressed against the tree like Micha could attack him at
any second.

For his part, Micha seemed more focused on playing
teacher and explaining the world of the supernatural to a
couple of uneducated youngsters who were too modern

for their own good.

"It means a lot. Both of you have abilities, abilities you can't explain. Evie, you've been surrounded by signs your entire life. I don't know what they mean yet, but I'd be willing to bet after last night they're connected to the power shifts going on in the universe. And you, Adam—you were able to sense me. You may not have realized it was me, but I know you knew I was there. And you're also the first person other than Evie to see me. Ever. I think that means you have a place in all of this."

"This is nuts. I'm out of here," Adam said, rising from his seat. "I've gone completely bonkers. I must have hit my head last night. That's got to be it."

"Then tell me where your spirit guide is," Micha challenged.

Adam stopped. "What are you talking about?"

"Everyone has a guide and a guardian, spirits who watch over them. So why am I the only one you can see? I'm not even attached to you, I'm attached to Evie. But even she can't see her spirit guide. I can see her. And I can see yours. And I know you know they're there, just like you could sense me, and just like you can sense the ghost of a little girl who lives in your apartment. She likes to move things, doesn't she? Especially your keys, or anything shiny you leave out on the counter. And she likes the wind chimes in the living room."

"How do you know about that?" Adam demanded. Equal parts fear and anger warred for dominance on his face. He looked like he didn't know if he should punch Micha or run away screaming.

"Chris told me. He's your spirit guide. He agrees with me." Micha approached him.

Frozen in place, Adam's eyes went wide as Micha whispered something in his ear.

"No. No way."

"Think about it." Micha stepped back so that he could see us both. "Somehow, the three of us have been drawn into this. I don't know what it means yet, but I think both of you are in danger." *Especially you.* The words hung unspoken when he looked at me.

"Whatever attacked Evie last night attacked you, too. It got your blood." He pointed to a scratch on Adam's cheek. He had more just like it on his arms, with a couple of bandages over the deeper cuts. "It'll come back for you. Just watch. Do you want to be caught with your pants down, or do you want to know who's behind it?"

Very slowly, Adam retook his seat. His dinner was a forgotten mess on the bench beside him, a victim of overexcited gesticulation. Throughout their exchange, I'd munched on my own, barely taking my eyes off them.

Balling up the empty wrapper, I stuck it back in the plastic bag. "So what's your plan, then? Go around knocking on grave stones until we find the gate to the Underworld, and then ask Hekate what's going on?"

"No. The two of you need a crash course in mythology and magic, first. Both of you need to get better at controlling your abilities. Then we need to figure out who is after you, and why. And try to find a way to convince them you're not a threat."

"Ce n'est pas nécessaire."

Like a herd of cats following a laser pointer, we all turned at once at the sound of the gravelly female voice.

It was the Dragon Lady from Dr. A's office. She stood on the path in her orthopedic shoes, arms crossed over her ample chest, with a cigarette pinched between two fingers.

"What are you doing here?" I asked.

She rolled her eyes at me and switched to English,

French condescension dripping from every syllable. "I come on behalf of the Sisterhood. You have been marked. Your soul was claimed millennia ago, and will be collected."

"What are you talking about? Collected by who?"

"You have the gift of Athena, Arachne's daughter. This gift was stolen, and it will be returned, for the glory of the goddess."

"Listen, I have no idea what you are talking about."

She sniffed, dropping her cigarette and stamping it out with her toe. "Changing forms will only protect you for so long. We will always find you, and when we do, we will take it back."

"Hi, can you even hear me? I don't know what you're talking about." I waved my hands at her, but she just rolled her eyes again. "I'm not changing forms, and I'm not going anywhere."

I might as well have been talking to the tree behind me.

"You have been marked by Athena. The Sisterhood will come for you, to collect what is rightfully ours. You have twenty-four hours to decide if you will willingly relinquish your powers, or if they will be taken by force."

"It's like talking to a brick wall," I said to no one in particular. "Would you mind starting over—"

Micha placed a hand on my arm. He shook his head, pulling me back a step.

"Don't bother. She's just a messenger," he said.

The Dragon Lady seemed to feel her message had been delivered, however cryptic it was, and turned and walked away, lighting another cigarette as she went.

"What's the Sisterhood? What's she even talking about?" Adam asked. It was good to know that I wasn't the only one who was confused.

"I imagine they're the modern followers of Athena," Micha replied. "They've gone by a few different names over the years."

"So you've run into them before?"

"A couple of times. They usually don't bother with warnings, though."

I gestured for him to elaborate, but he didn't. I could see the worry on his features. It bled from his hand into mine where we touched.

Adam's face tightened with worry. "This is bad, isn't it? What do they want Evie for?"

Micha's brow furrowed. "That's the part I've never been able to understand."

# Chapter Six
## Story Time

I was late getting home. Izzy acted nonchalant, but I could tell she was relieved. "I'm sorry it took so long. I ran into a friend and we got caught up talking," I said, kicking off my shoes and leaving them by the door.

"That's fine. I'm putting in a movie. Do you want to watch it with me?" She held up the first *Lord of the Rings* DVD.

I had to think about it. I had a date with Google, but there was no reason why my research couldn't overlap with Frodo, Legolas, and a big bag of microwave popcorn.

Besides, I'd been spending a lot of time in my room. Izzy wouldn't force me to talk to her if I didn't want to, but part of our unspoken deal was spending time together—it was one of the reasons I'd come to Montreal in the first place.

"Sure. Just let me grab my laptop."

"I'll start the popcorn."

By the time we'd gotten the *Cliff's Notes* version of the One Ring's history, I was on the couch with my half of the popcorn and half a dozen webpages open, sifting through bad grammar and clipart for information on Athena and the Sisterhood.

"What are you working on?" Izzy asked. She'd already put her laptop away for the day. She wasn't much of a crafter, but she'd started crocheting again after I came to stay with her. I had no idea what she was working on. It kind of looked like an octopus. She'd claimed it was a hat when I asked. I was doubtful, but let it drop.

"Just looking into something a friend mentioned." An idea. "Hey, what do you know about Athena?"

"The goddess?" Izzy hit pause on the remote. "Well, she's a goddess who sprang out of Zeus's head when he had a headache. She's the patron of war, architecture, and weaving, and is one of several virgin goddesses—not a fan of men at all. She's also one of the more vindictive goddesses in that pantheon. She turned Medusa into a Gorgon when she was raped by Poseidon in her temple— Poseidon got off scot-free on that one, of course—and she turned Arachne into a spider when she beat her at a weaving contest."

"Wait, you mean Arachne won the contest?"

"Well, it depends on which version you read. In some of them, Athena wins and punishes Arachne for her pride and boasting. In others, Arachne is a very ungracious winner, and that's why she gets cursed. But either way, Athena is a fan of turning people into creepy crawlies when they cross her. She's big on her curses. Why?"

"Something I heard. I'm just curious. What about Arachne's family? Did Athena ever do anything to them?"

Izzy shrugged. "They aren't mentioned in most of the myths. Though I did read one version where Athena placed a curse on Arachne's entire family, and her husband gave up their daughter as an offering to placate her."

*Arachne's daughter.* "What happened to her?"

Izzy shrugged. "I don't remember. I only came across that retelling once, a long time ago. Hey, try looking up the Athenian Society. They've got all kinds of mythology info on their website. Some of the versions they have are pretty different from the standard myths."

I typed it in quickly.

Izzy went back to the movie.

My screen filled with a photo of a classical revival building and expertly manicured grounds. The caption listed it as the headquarters for the Athenian Sisterhood, Chicago, Illinois.

Micha appeared at my side. We exchanged looks. *No way*, I thought. No way could it be that easy. I glanced over at Izzy, but she was absorbed in the movie. Was this really the Sisterhood that Dragon Lady was talking about?

I started with the *About* section. They described themselves as a women's fellowship, dedicated to promoting education, independent thought, and professional enhancement for women all over the world.

The whole thing sounded like one of the pamphlets my high school guidance office supplied, and made me want to gag a little. The site showed happy, smiling women dressed in their business best, posing with books, microscopes, and blueprints. Membership was listed as a "bargain" at only five hundred dollars for a year. I snorted.

*Well, they don't seem like the black hood, human sacrifice types.* More like the rob-you-blind types.

Digging deeper into the site, I found information about scholarships offered for both members and nonmembers. Their biggest scholarship was twenty thousand dollars, open to textile artists.

"Well that's oddly specific," I said, clicking on the link.

"What is?" Izzy asked.

"Nothing. Just reading."

According to the description, the prize was only open every two years. And all you had to do to win, was weave.

"Yeah, I think this is them," Micha said. "That doesn't sound like they're trying to track down someone related to Arachne at all. Not even remotely suspicious."

I bit my tongue to keep from replying out loud, and instead dove into their Sources page, like my aunt had recommended. I found list upon list of myths from all over the world, but primarily Greece. The introduction at the top of the page described their Chicago headquarters as having one of the largest libraries of mythology texts in the world. "At Athens, we believe that by looking at the lessons of the past in the form of oral history, myth, and legend, we can build a solid, more creative future."

I couldn't even believe what I was reading. "These people are nuts."

From her chair, Izzy snorted. "You should try talking to some of them in person." I raised an eyebrow. "Back when I was attending university, I was approached by them and asked to join. At first it sounded pretty good, and at the time I could use all the help I could get, but after sitting through the first meeting I realized they were all completely cracked. It was like Girl Guides for grownups, but with kool-aide instead of cookies. I got thrown out after three meetings. I didn't play well with others. I didn't see things ending well if I signed on their dotted line."

"I'm amazed you even got that far. Five hundred dollars?"

Izzy snorted. "Is that what they're charging the professionals now? No, they had a student rate when I was in school. Fifty dollars to apply, then twenty-five dollars or something a year after that. Which was still kind of a lot back then, but they offered a lot of scholarships and stuff. They seem to do good things from what I can tell, they're just…weird."

"Yeah, I noticed."

"You should hear one of their recruiters talk sometime. I think my old literature professor is still connected to them. She was the one who recruited me, back in the day. Actually, I think she was the one who told me the weird version of Athena and Arachne." Izzy looked thoughtful for a moment. "You know…I think I still have that book. Let me check." She popped up from her chair and went to her office to retrieve it. When she came back, it was with a spiral-bound book with a clear plastic cover. The pages were typewritten with hand drawn illustrations, Xeroxed, and then bound at a copy store.

"She actually wrote the book for her own class?"

"Yeah. Well, one of them. We had another regular textbook we used. This was just for a special unit she was doing. I don't even remember what it was on. The only reason I kept the damn thing is because there's a section in the back where she talks about effective storytelling, and that bit struck a chord with me. I guess that was when I decided I was going to write for a living. Well, either then or when I got fired from McDonalds."

The eyebrow went up again.

Izzy shrugged. "I had a problem with authority when I was your age."

I raised my other eyebrow.

"What? I never said it changed. What's with the sudden interest, anyway?"

"Oh, it's nothing. I just heard a couple of people talking about it at work the other day and wanted to find out what it was about." The ancient plastic in the book cover creaked when I opened it and began scanning the first pages.

The movie was already more than half over, and I'd missed most of it because of my research. "I think I'll just go read for a bit," I said, taking it back to my room.

With the door closed, I flopped down on the bed, spreading the book open on my pillow.

***

The next time I looked up, it was almost midnight. Blinking and stretching, I felt my back and shoulders pop. I wasn't sure how long I'd been lying there.

At over fifty pages, Dr. Madge Kelly's retelling of Arachne was a far cry from your standard short story. Dark and ominous, it had more in common with Dracula than the myths I remembered reading in grade school.

The core of the story was still the same: Arachne, a young, talented weaver, boasted she was better than everyone else, including the gods. Athena, disguised as an old woman, warned her to mind her manners, but Arachne refused and challenged the old woman instead. When Arachne lost, Athena revealed herself and punished the prideful girl.

Except in Kelly's version, that was only the beginning of the story.

Athena blessed Arachne's family generations before, but Arachne herself took the talent as her own and credited neither her family nor the gods. She claimed it was her own skill that allowed her to manipulate the threads the way she did.

After her crushing defeat and transfiguration into a spider, Athena started to place a curse on the entire family and all of their descendants. Arachne's husband, however, begged her to reconsider, stating he would use the wealth they had amassed through his wife's sought-after weavings to build her a magnificent shrine. He would dedicate his daughter, his first-born, as her servant, offering up her talents for the glory of Athena.

The goddess considered his offer, and finally accepted. She would spare their lives. Immediately, he set to work on the shrine. It grew into a vast temple. He allocated slaves for its upkeep, and even attracted a priestess and several local girls who became dedicated to the goddess.

When construction was complete, he planned a grand ceremony to turn his daughter over to the care of the priestess. But the night before, one of his slaves—having seen what Athena did to Arachne in her rage—stole away with the child, traveling far to the south, to the islands dotting the Aegean.

The slave, however, was an old woman, and not suited for long travel. She grew ill on the road and had to stop at a small, remote village.

Coming to a temple at a crossroads, the old woman collapsed. The priestesses rushed out to aide her, but the elderly slave died shortly thereafter, leaving the nameless infant behind.

The little girl grew up in the temple, taken in by the priestesses. She worked as their servant, until her powers were discovered, and the High Priestess decided to use them for her own benefit. Under her coercion, the girl used her abilities for the benefit of the temple, which grew prosperous. Her bandages miraculously healed wounds. A cloak made from her fabric was rumored to protect a soldier from harm. She used the gifts of Athena to create trivial charms for the people of the village, and in doing so, drew attention to herself.

Athena, once again in the guise of an old woman, appeared on the doorstep of the temple—late one night when only the girl was awake, manning the flame that was kept burning for travelers. When the old woman saw her work, she asked if she was a servant of Athena, but the girl only laughed.

"No, I am a dedicated to Hekate, of the Underworld," she replied.

"But your talents could serve so many more if you were part of a temple of Athena. Her reach is far greater than Hekate's."

"Nothing reaches farther than death," said the girl. "And were I to become dedicated to Athena, I would have to give up my betrothed."

"Surely a man is not worth more than the good you could do for others," Athena pressed.

"Perhaps. But I think we can do more good together."

Angered by her response, Athena wanted to curse the girl, but found that Hekate had blessed her, and she could not so long as she was inside the other goddess' temple.

Not to be discouraged, Athena turned to a neighboring kingdom. In a dream, she told the king of the great wealth hiding just beyond his reach, and of the girl with the mystical powers. "Give the girl to me, and you shall have the rest," Athena commanded.

The king sent his troops to the village, ordering them to give up the girl. But she was nowhere to be found. She and her lover hid, and watched as the village burned to ashes. When the soldiers found her, they executed her lover, and took her to the king. But before they could make it back to the castle, she killed her guards, placing a curse upon the kingdom, before jumping to her death, preventing Athena from taking back what was rightfully hers—her powers.

The whole thing just sounded so crazy—and yet, there were enough similarities to what I'd seen under hypnosis to make me wonder. It wasn't accurate. Not in the least. But I could see, maybe, someone else viewing events that way. For example, another party who thought they had been wronged?

Or, a vengeful, bitchy goddess, to paraphrase Izzy.

I yawned, pushing the book aside. If Izzy was right, and this was the version of the myth the Sisterhood was using, and they'd pegged me as the villain in their little story, then what exactly did it mean? And what was I going to do about it?

Before I could contemplate it too deeply, however, I fell asleep.

# Chapter Seven
## Back to School

I woke up the next morning with my face pressed into the spiral binding of the textbook. Some of the ink had transferred onto my cheek, and I had a hell of a time scrubbing it off in the shower. Finally, I was dressed, medicated, and with toast in hand I ran out the door to catch my train to work.

The bookshop was the last place I wanted to be, but I had to admit it had its advantages. Under the pretense of organizing the department and dusting the shelves, I spent the first half of my shift sifting through books on mythology and Ancient Greece, searching for any clues that might lead back to the Sisterhood and what exactly they had planned. All of my sources came up dry, though. I even flipped through a copy of *Secret Societies and Symbols* with no luck. It seemed the Athenian Society wasn't on anyone's radar, at least not in print.

When I got back from my break, Adam was leaning against the computer terminal on the second floor.

"What are you doing here?" I asked. "Your books won't be in for at least a few more days."

"I know. I was in the area and thought I'd see if you

were working. And if maybe you wanted to grab lunch."

Caught off guard by the suggestion, I answered without thinking. "Why?"

"Um, because I want to talk to you? And because it's generally what you do with friend-type people."

"Are we friend-type people?" He seemed so uncertain around me it was hard to tell. Not that I blamed him.

"I figure if you survive being mauled by vicious owls together, spend two nights in a row in a graveyard together—one of them involving food and drink—and are threatened by the same creepy old lady, then yes, you are friend-type people. Possibly even actual friends."

I responded to his smile in kind. "In that case, I would love to go to lunch. But I've still got two hours left on my shift."

"Not a problem. I was going to check out the fiction section, anyway. There are a couple of new releases I want to pick up."

"Well, then why don't I show you where they are?" I said, putting on my best hostess voice and gesturing for him to follow me back to the first floor.

We chatted about books for a while, until I caught my boss watching me and figured I'd played out the "helpful associate" card. Sheesh. First I'm in trouble for not being friendly, and then she was giving me the stink eye for being *too* friendly. Some days you can't please anyone.

When my shift was finally over, I met Adam in front of the store. He was holding a giant bag with the store logo printed on the front.

"Holy crap, what did you buy? Do we even have anything left?" I asked.

Adam laughed. "What can I say? I like to read. I only buy books a couple times a year, so I tend to get a lot of them. These'll keep me set for the next few months."

"You know, there's this thing called a *library*."

"Shush. I'm paying your wage."

"In that case, I demand a raise."

We went down to the lowest level of the mall, where the food court connected back to the McGill Metro station. Splitting up temporarily, we selected our fare and then met back at a table near the fountain dominating the middle of the shopping center.

Still lugging his giant bag, Adam had a cheeseburger, poutine, and a milkshake precariously balanced on a green plastic tray. Every time he moved, they slid to one side or the other, threatening to topple onto the nearest passerby at any second.

My tray was already safely on the laminate table and I was tucking into a gyro. "Oh, a milkshake. I should have gotten one of those." Milkshakes are practically a food group for me.

"There's still time," Adam said, his own sliding to the right, then quickly to the front as he set the tray down.

Around us, conversations in English, French, Korean, Spanish, and German bounced off the marble tiles, mingling with the sound of falling water. Laughter echoed from somewhere above, and the flash of a camera reflected on polished metal and glass; a tourist marking their time in Montreal.

Malls hadn't had much appeal to me when I lived in Toronto, probably because I wasn't one of those mall-trolling types; I was the stay-at-home-with-yarn type, and that didn't go over so well in most social circles. But the Underground City was different.

A massive network of shopping centers, pricey high rise condos and office buildings, the RESO, as it was officially called—a play on a French word meaning "network"—was different. It was a meeting place, a travel hub. In a city that spent six months of the year buried under snow, it was a place where even in the coldest weather people could gather comfortably to talk, share, and commune. It was entirely possible to live, work, and play within the network and not go outside all winter, since it covered most of downtown and was even connected to some of the civic buildings.

Adam's voice brought me out of my daydream. "So is your, ah, friend here?" He sounded uncertain of the term.

"Oh, you mean Micha?" I asked after a minute, trying to catch his train of thought. "Yeah. He's always around."

"So you can like, see him?"

I shrugged. "Not at the moment, but I know he's there. Kind of like you know when someone is reading over your shoulder. He's never *not* there, but he's trying to be unobtrusive."

"What does that mean?"

"It means instead of just sitting there like a normal person, he's a flash in the corner of my eye, the one where you might have seen something, but you're not sure. Kind of, anyway."

"That sounds annoying."

"It is. But I'm getting used to it. For weeks after he first showed up, he wouldn't go away for anything. He kept watching me, and talking to me. I kept trying to ignore him so that people wouldn't see me talking to myself and think I was nuts."

"All the time? Even…like, in the bathroom?"

"Well, not quite. But he was always waiting outside." Bastard. That had been really annoying. No privacy, whatsoever. Not that there's a lot of it to begin with in a psych ward.

Adam opened his mouth to ask another question, then seemed to think better of it. "How… Well, I guess, when…."

"When did I start seeing him?" I guessed.

He nodded.

I put down my gyro. I tried to find the words. I tried to find the strength to say them. *I tried to kill myself. I spent three months in a mental hospital, trying to convince them I was sane while at the same time I was being followed around by a guy only I could see and hear.*

"I plead the fifth on this one," I said at last. "Maybe some other time."

"I'm sorry, I shouldn't have asked. I knew it had to be pretty personal."

"Let's just say I had a trauma. A near-death experience, if you will. And when I woke up, he was there. And he hasn't left since."

Adam nodded, accepting the answer. Then he quickly changed the subject: "So what did you make of the crazy lady last night? I haven't been able to get her out of my head. I mean, how did she even know you were there?"

"She's probably been following me. She's the receptionist at…" I paused. I'd never said the words out loud to anyone. My family knew, of course, but I'd never actually told anyone.

"At..?"

"My therapist's office." I mumbled the words around a big bite of lamb and cucumber sauce.

"What?"

I swallowed. "My shrink."

"Oh. Okay." Adam seemed unphased. Well, I guess he wouldn't be, as a psychology student.

"I think she must have listened in on my last session." I gave him the short version of the hypnosis. "She's never shown an interest in me before, and that's the first time anything really weird has happened, so that must be it."

"Do you know what the sisterhood she kept talking about was?"

I told him about my research the night before. "They seem to be pretty low-key, more the women behind the curtain types, but I could be wrong. From what Izzy told me, it sounds like they've changed a lot since she was in school."

"What university did your aunt go to?"

"Concordia." It was the smaller of the two English universities in Quebec, but had a little more of an arts focus, while McGill was geared more toward science and math.

Adam chewed thoughtfully on a fry, gravy dripping onto his tray. "I wonder if she's still there."

"Who?"

"Her old teacher. Maybe we should pay her a visit."

***

One Metro stop and a short walk later, and we were on campus. After a little mindless wandering, we found the admin building and inquired about Dr. Kelly. We were in luck. Her last class of the day was wrapping up just a few buildings over.

The door of room 302 was open. I could hear a woman's voice, lecturing on the merits of a work of fiction, quoting bits and pieces of a story I'd never heard of.

Adam and I slipped into two empty seats at the back of the room while her attention was on the whiteboard, drawing lines between character names and places. When she turned around and saw us in the back, she skipped a beat in her speech, but kept going. The hiccup was so slight I doubt anyone but Adam and I would have noticed—except for the fact her eyes zoomed in on me like a hunter putting a twelve-point buck in his crosshairs with a laser sight.

I shifted nervously in my seat, feeling like an impostor. I'd only made it through the first month of classes before everything fell apart. To be honest, I barely even remembered it, other than the crushing waves of anxiety that followed me everywhere, and the feeling I would never, ever, make it through. I hadn't even made it one semester before dropping out. *What a loser. I couldn't—*

Micha's hand on my shoulder. He stood behind me, leaning down to whisper in my ear. "You didn't fail. You might be damaged, but you're not broken. You just weren't meant to be there at that time, in that place. When you're better, you can try again. Maybe this fall," he suggested.

I nodded, fighting back tears. I reached up to take his hand, hoping no one noticed.

Adam, of course, did. He gave me a confused look. "Are you okay?" he mouthed.

"Fine," I whispered, backhanding moisture from my eyes. Dammit, why did everything have to bring me to tears?

"Don't forget, the final exam is tomorrow morning. If you haven't turned in your papers to me by now, you're out of luck!" she called, almost cheerfully, as the students packed up their bags and filed out of the room.

I followed Adam to the lectern. My sudden bout of emotion had me feeling shy. I would have happily fled the room or vanished into the floor had the opportunity presented itself. Adam looked over his shoulder at me. I took a deep breath and tried to act like a normal person and not an escaped lunatic.

"You have got to be Isabella Cappelli's daughter," Kelly said, locking eyes with me. I tried not to squirm under her scrutiny.

"Niece, actually," I corrected. "But everyone says that." I looked like a taller, younger version of Izzy, though her eyes were more of a grey color and mine were more of a very pale blue. Same olive complexion, same dark hair and classic Italian features. My grandmother said we looked like the Mona Lisa—quiet, secretive. We might have been considered pretty in another time and place, but neither of us was going to get nominated Miss Canada any time soon. The polite name for our features was "hawk-like."

"I was so surprised to see you there, I thought you were her for a minute," Dr. Kelly continued. "How is Izzy? I don't think I've spoken to her since she graduated. She sent me one of her books a few years ago. It was…interesting."

"She's good. She just found out last month one of her books is being made into a movie." I shoved my hands into my pockets to keep from fidgeting. Something about Dr. Kelly made the hair on the back of my neck stand on end, but I had no idea why. She was polite and professional, and didn't seem at all out of place. But I couldn't shake the feeling that if she moved, I would find something sinister grinning at me from just over her shoulder.

"Dr. Kelly, Izzy is actually the one who gave us your name. I'm a student at McGill, and I'm thinking of transferring, and Evie here is still looking at where she wants to enroll. We heard such good things about you we thought we'd come meet you while we look around campus." Bless Adam, his empathy, and his ability to take control.

The teacher looked slightly taken off guard. "Oh. Well, I don't think I'm really the one you want to talk to about that. Maybe someone in admissions or guidance would be better able to answer your questions."

"Well, we were interested in the teaching style here. The classes are so much smaller. I was really intrigued by your lecture."

Flattered, Dr. Kelly offered Adam a smile. "Are you familiar with Julia Kavanagh?"

"No, but I think I'd like to be."

Okay, we were starting to border on flirting now, which was just getting creepy. Adam did realize she was old enough to be his grandmother, right?

"Izzy mentioned there was a society here you were involved in. I wanted to know if it was still around," I blurted. I winced at my own awkwardness.

Dr. Kelly turned her attention back to me, blue eyes blinking owlishly at me from behind thick black frames. "Really? I'm surprised. Izzy turned down our invitation."

"That's what she said. But I was looking at the website, and I wondered if you could tell me more about it."

She packed up her briefcase thoughtfully. "Well, for starters you have to have a recommendation from an existing elder to be nominated for membership into the Sisterhood. Second, you must have an excellent academic record. What are your grades like?" We followed her out the door, walking slowly as we talked.

I bit the inside of my cheek. "I had to leave school last year. I had…I had some health problems. But they're mostly under control now."

"Hm. Yes." Was she judging me? Her eyes swept me up and down, lips pursed. Then she turned a similar disapproving look on Adam. "Well, we can work around that. I remember Izzy was in a similar situation when I first met her. But so long as you can recover from those setbacks and prove you are willing to work and here to learn, I think we can find a way around that.

"The Athenian Society is only open to women, of course," She glanced over at Adam.

"Is there a version for guys?" I asked, genuinely curious.

"No. But if you're really interested, I can put you in contact with several excellent academic organizations."

"That would be great," my friend said graciously.

"Have you put in your application yet?"

I shook my head. "I'm still kind of deciding what I want to do and where I want to go. Like I said, I haven't really been well for the last couple of months."

Dr. Kelly nodded, the disapproving look back on her face. "Well, you need to decide quickly. The deadlines for fall term are already over, but you might be able to get in for the winter semester if you're lucky. Do you have any idea of your major?"

My parents wanted me to major in business or something practical like that. "I'm torn between creative writing and maybe art or fashion. Something with fibers." My mother would have a fit if she heard me say I wanted to study not just art, but textile art, out loud. My dad wouldn't say anything—he'd be too busy having a stroke.

Our new acquaintance smiled broadly. "Very like your aunt, aren't you?"

"What do you mean?"

"I had Izzy as a first year. She was dead set on studying costume design through our theater program, but after reading a few of her assignments, I couldn't let her waste her talents there. It took the better part of two semesters, but I finally convinced her that her real gift was for the written word."

"She said it was your class that made her want to be a writer."

Dr. Kelly flushed a little. She waved off the praise. "Well. I was just doing my job as her teacher." We'd reached the bottom of the staircase, and a door opened onto the first floor. "I need to be off. But if you need anything," she produced a business card from one of the outer pockets of her leather bag. "The Athenian Society is having a gathering tomorrow night. It might be a good idea for you to come, get a better idea of what we're about." Another of her quick glances at Adam. "Ladies only, of course."

"Of course." I smiled tightly, hoping my discomfort didn't spread to my eyes as I tucked her card into my back pocket. "Thanks so much for your help."

"Any time." She wiggled her fingers at us before vanishing out the door.

"What do you think?" I asked Adam.

"Well, she's completely manipulative, and very conceited. Are you really going to go to their thing?"

"I don't know. Tomorrow's my birthday. I'm supposed to spend it with Izzy."

"Tomorrow's your birthday? Why didn't you say something?"

I raised one shoulder and let it drop. "I haven't felt like celebrating. It was Izzy's idea." I found the idea of going to a party—any party—to be repulsive. Especially if it was going to be populated with the Dragon Lady, Dr. Kelly, and a hundred of their closest friends.

"They know who you are, and they just happen to be having a big to-do tomorrow night. That doesn't sound like a trap, now does it?"

"Now just because Dr. Kelly and that receptionist are a little weird doesn't mean they're up to no good," I said. "I mean, we could be barking up the completely wrong tree here. Maybe it's all just a bunch of weird coincidences, and this will just be like some sorority get together like you see in the movies, and they'll all wear pink glitter and paint each other's nails." My brain tried to insert the image of Dr. Kelly and her short gray pixie cut and black pantsuit into the opening scene from *Legally Blond* with minimal success.

"You don't really believe that, do you?"

"Not a chance."

# Chapter Eight
## Party with the Enemy

After a brief exchange with Dr. Kelly via email, I got the location and dress code for the gathering. It was, in fact, a party to celebrate that year's graduating class and to give the current students a chance to rub elbows with professional members.

I had no idea what to wear. I called Adam to ask his advice, but he was absolutely no help, suggesting I wear "clothes."

"Thanks, Captain Obvious. Suggest something like that again, and I'll make you come shopping with me."

"Too bad. I'm in class all day. Finals. Oops, would you look at the time? My lunch break is almost over. 'Bye."

And then the bastard hung up on me.

Asking Izzy didn't go much better, since first I had to tell her I was skipping our low-key movie and take-out evening to go party with the crazy people she'd subtly been warning me about the night before.

"I'm not sure how I feel about you going to this thing," she said, watching me try on clothes from her closet.

After months of stress and medication messing with

my appetite, I was way too skinny. Most of my clothes hung loosely, at least two or three sizes too big. Which meant I was just thin enough to fit into petite Izzy's clothes. The problem was I was a head taller, which made the red number I was trying on go from nice to naughty in two seconds flat. The hem was barely long enough to reach my palm.

"Me neither. Maybe I shouldn't go." My nerves were back in full force. What was I thinking? The past few days had been crazy, sure, but somehow my brain had made all kinds of illogical leaps. There was no proof Dr. Kelly or anyone else wanted me harmed—well, except maybe the Dragon Lady. I really needed to find out her name…and get a new shrink. So why was I crashing a party with a bunch of egotistical whack jobs anyway?

For the millionth time, I wished Adam were going. Micha was one thing, but it would be nice to have a solid, masculine presence to hide behind. Especially since he seemed to have a knack for buttering up Kelly. Which might come in handy if I made as big of an ass of myself as I suspected I would.

Speaking of, my spirit companion was still trying to keep his distance. I saw his faint reflection in the mirror as I tried to tug the hemline a little lower without exposing cleavage. Hazy, like an image on the surface of a pond, he flickered in and out. Watching me, but trying to keep me from noticing him.

His avoidance made me feel even less enthused. After months of trying so hard to pretend he wasn't there, I'd finally started to get to know him, and now he was pulling away.

The conscious part of my brain that had been going through months and months of therapy understood why and supplied a litany of reasons. I needed to make human connections—I couldn't live in my head. And I needed to form an attachment to someone that wasn't completely codependent; even I could see Micha and I had already come to depend on each other far more than was healthy.

But another part of me missed him, and felt rejected by the distance. Even if my brain recognized the reasoning, the rest of me was still sinking at the thought of not being good enough. If I were better, somehow, then he wouldn't pull away. Then it wouldn't hurt. I wouldn't—

I shook my head. I couldn't be thinking about those things. Not now.

*You can get through this. It's not something you did. It's for your own good. You'll benefit from this in the long run—*

"That's it, I'm coming with you."

"What?"

"I don't like this. Take that off." Izzy reached into her closet and tossed something longer, swooshier, and black at me. "This one. You do have heels, right?"

I unzipped the little red dress. "You don't have to come—"

"Yes, I do. If there's one thing I remember about Dr. Kelly, it's that she has a way of twisting people's words and the way they think. And she won't let a subject drop once she's gotten it into her head."

"Why do I get the feeling this is like one of those high school reunion things, where you want to show off to all the people who rejected you?"

"Hey, I said no to them, remember?" Izzy grabbed the red dress with one hand, pulling her worn T-shirt over her head with the other. Her lips pressed into a thin line. "Look, if this really means that much to you, then go for it. They've got a lot of great connections, and it might help you down the road. But I want you to know you are under no obligation to live up to their expectations. You're an awesome kid. Young lady. Woman. Whatever. And you're going to do awesome things, whether they help you or not."

I couldn't help blushing. Izzy's pep talks were always so aggressive. You *will* do this, and you *will* be great at it. My mom's version of encouragement was usually to tell me about all of the horrible things that would happen if I failed, and how I needed to do well, no matter what.

Just thinking about it, and what she would say to me at that moment, made me want to hyperventilate.

The second dress fit a lot better than the first. Mid-calf on Izzy, it fell to just below my knees. Sleeveless, V-necked, and fitted through the thigh before flaring out. And black. Most of my wardrobe was black, because apparently I live to be a cliché. Much more my speed, though I still rubbed at my scars self-consciously.

The hair on the back of my neck prickled from the pressure of Micha's semi-visible gaze. I turned around and felt my cheeks color again. Izzy didn't notice. She was already leaning over her vanity, applying concealer under her eyes.

I mumbled something about shoes and ran back to my room. I had my choice of flip-flops, red Chuck Taylors, combat boots, snow boots, or a pair of strappy sandals with a spindly four-inch heel.

I was tempted to go with the sneakers or the combat boots, but once again my mom's voice in the back of my head stopped me. Reluctantly, I pulled out the heels. I could barely walk in them and knew I would have blisters by the end of the night, but this was one thing I would not be able to borrow from Izzy.

"I can see you, you know," I said, buckling one of the

straps around my ankle. In the far reaches of my vision, Micha twitched, but didn't vanish. He started to say something, but the ring of my cell phone cut him off. He disappeared before I'd even managed to pick up.

*Speak of the devil.* My mom's picture flashed on the screen.

"Hi, Mom," I said, cradling the phone with my shoulder while I struggled to buckle my other shoe. Only worn once for a cousin's wedding, the holes were just big enough to accommodate the prong of the buckle.

"Hi, sweetie! I just wanted to wish you a happy birthday!" Her voice was entirely too cheerful for me at the moment, but it was still good to hear.

I realized suddenly that I'd actually missed my parents. It came as something as a shock, considering how much we argued.

"So how are you spending your special day?"

"Just going out with Izzy tonight. Nothing too special."

"Well, well I hope you enjoy yourself. I sent you a package with your birthday present and a few little things I thought you could use. It hasn't shown up yet, has it?"

"No, but I'll keep an eye out for it." *Got it.* Strapped into place, I put my foot back on the floor and lay down on the bed. Comfy bed. I hadn't been seeing enough of it lately. As soon as this party was over, I was going to spend a long time getting reacquainted with it.

Mom's voice took on an uncertain quality. "Do you know yet when you might be coming home?"

*Ah. Here we go.* "Not yet, Mom. I like it here."

"Well, you can't impose on your aunt forever. And didn't you say you were doing better? Isn't it time for you to come home, and go back to school? It's been months now."

I pinched the bridge of my nose. "I have a job here, Mom. And I'm looking at schools in Montreal."

"But why there? You know we have dozens of excellent schools, right here. What does Montreal have? Only one school that's really worth note."

"Mom, there are at least three really good schools here. Concordia is excellent with sciences—"

"But you won't be studying science, now will you? You barely made it through biology, and we had to get that tutor so you could pass algebra. And your tuition would be higher, since you're technically still a resident of Ontario, and the health care is better here, too. You really shouldn't be making your dad pay out-of-pocket for all of those sessions when they would be free here."

I tried to swallow my doubts and remember the affirmations and the reasoning I had worked out with Dr. A. I'd practiced the speech in my head. It was supposed to help relieve some of my anxiety, since I'd already been through her list of reasons to go back to Toronto every time she'd called. "You know what Mom, I don't feel like arguing about this right now. I'm fine where I am. I'm trying to save some money so I'm not dependent on Izzy, and I'm trying to make things better for myself."

"You can do that here."

"I'll talk to you later."

I hung up over her objections, tossing the phone down on my pillow.

Great. As if my confidence wasn't already in the gutter over this stupid party, now I had my mother's criticisms echoing in my brain.

It was just like when I came home after the hospital. Every conversation, no matter how trivial, turned into an argument. If I was depressed, then it was because I wasn't trying hard enough. If I felt fine that day, then clearly there was never anything wrong and I needed to stop complaining and exaggerating everything. I was over dramatic, nasty, and inconsiderate of others.

My list of faults played over and over. I covered my eyes, but couldn't block it out.

Izzy knocked lightly on my doorframe. I peered out at her through my fingers.

"Hey, kiddo. Was that Margaret?"

I nodded, closing my eyes again. The worst part was knowing Mom was right. I was crashing in Izzy's guest room, eating her food, interrupting her work—

She sat down next to me. "You know, Margaret's a great woman. She's tough, you know? She has to be to put up with my brother. But she tends to spend way too much time worrying about what other people think, and not enough time worrying about the people who actually matter. She likes to think she can read people's minds, but really it's all in her head."

I lowered my hands. "Were you listening or something?"

Izzy shrugged, one corner of her mouth twitching upward. "We've gotten into enough fights over the years that I know her style." She touched my hair, just once. "She's worried about you. You're her baby girl, and you've been gone a long time. She misses you."

"She's got a funny way of showing it," I grumbled.

"She's just trying to do what's best for you. She wanted to keep you near and take care of you, but in the end she knew it was best to send you away. That's one of the hardest decisions for a parent to make." For a second, I though Izzy's eyes looked misty, but she blinked it away quickly.

"Then why does it always feel like she's doing what's best for her?"

Izzy pulled me into a hug. With my head on her shoulder, I could smell her perfume. It was a familiar scent, like one I'd smelled a long time ago and now couldn't place. "Be patient with her, honey. She's doing her best. Having a kid doesn't always mean you know what to do in every situation, and your situation is kinda sticky right now. Better, but still sticky. I think having space has been good for both of you. When you're ready, though, she'll be there when you reach out again."

Heaving a sigh, I straightened. "Where were you when I was a kid? You're so much better at this mom thing than she is."

It was only a joke, but Izzy's face creased in what appeared to be pain for a split second before she forced a laugh. "Sweetheart, trust me. It's better for everyone that I'm your aunt and not your mom. I'm much better at the spoil-'em-rotten and turn-'em-loose routine than the whole teaching and discipline thing. And honestly, I think your mom has done a bang-up job. If it wasn't for her, you wouldn't be nearly so cool."

I snorted, wiping at my eyes. "Sure. I'll take your word for it."

"Come on. Enough of this. We still need to do your hair and makeup."

***

An hour later, Izzy and I climbed out of a cab in front of Hôtel Place d'Armes. The Jeep wasn't really suited to arriving in style, and no car was suited to parking downtown.

One of the biggest, fanciest hotels in Montreal, *intimidating* was something of an understatement. One of their cheaper rooms cost more per night than I made in a month.

The entryway was all white marble with black accents. I blended in with the floor tiles, which was something of a relief, but Izzy stood out, and she knew how to work it. I followed the tiny red skirt—which was just the right length on her—up to the front desk, where we got directions to the terrace. Izzy smiled at the man behind the counter, tossing her wrap a little higher on her shoulder. In response, he looked ready to melt into a puddle of goo on the floor.

"Is that the shawl I made you?" I fingered the fine black cobweb-weight yarn.

"Yep. I saw it in my drawer and thought it would be just perfect for tonight." I'd found the pattern online; it was a big circular beaded shawl called Spider's Web, and the stitch pattern lived up to the name. Izzy had secured it with a piece of rhinestone costume jewelry leftover from Halloween, in the shape of a spider.

"Going for irony, eh?"

"I thought it was appropriate. Besides, you got me thinking about that weird story of Dr. Kelly's. It just kind of seemed right."

The shawl had been a present for Izzy, a thank-you for letting me stay with her. At the time, I hadn't wanted to do anything—I was unmotivated, didn't want to find a job, and was completely paralyzed with doubt, so I was channeling all my uncertainty into my knitting. I knocked out a massive lace shawl in two weeks, and poured almost all the money I'd brought with me from Toronto into the silk and angora yarn. When I cast off, it felt like I could breathe for the first time in months.

Izzy had been completely giddy over the gift. Its completion left me hungry for another project, but with no money left to buy nice yarn, I had to get a job.

Periwinkle Books happened a few weeks later. For my aunt, that shawl might have meant hours of labor, the love of family, and a gorgeous accessory. For me, it was finally shaking off the dark cloud that had been following me, turning something awful into something beautiful, and beginning to move forward with my life.

I had grabbed some knitwear for myself, too. I couldn't leave my arms bare, so I pulled a pair of black arm warmers out of my drawer. They laced up with a satin ribbon and had ruffles that fell over my hands. Even in the heat of summer, I never went out without something to cover the scars. It wasn't that they bothered me, exactly, but the way other people reacted made me uncomfortable.

The elevator dinged and we exited onto the rooftop terrace. I sucked in a breath. Downtown spread out before us, painted in pinks and golds by the setting sun. The St. Laurence River cut an illuminated path to our right, reflecting the candy colors of the sky as it coursed eastward.

An outdoor café dominated the rooftop, covered by a striped overhang to keep the sun and rain off. Around the edge, a broad walkway offered an even better view of the city. The kitchen was closed, but a buffet was laid out against the wall, offering everything from champagne to mini vegan quiches and petite-fours with delicate little roses on them. A small stage had been set up in one corner. About fifty women in cocktail dresses gathered in front of it, ranging from my age to well into their eighties.

"Well, I guess we should find Dr. Kelly first and say hello," Izzy said, leading the way into the crowd.

I was more than happy to follow in her lead. The sight of the well-dressed group had me inches from panicking, remembering what an interloper I was. *I don't belong here. What was I thinking? I should just let the whole thing go....*

Micha looped his arm through mine. Usually, he appeared in jeans, a faded T-shirt, and a leather jacket, but tonight he'd turned it in for a tux, his curly hair smoothed back. The white strands above his forehead caught the sunset, reflecting fire red and brilliant gold.

I started to ask where the tux came from, but he shook his head.

"Shh," he whispered, leaning in close as if someone else might hear him. "I can appear however I want. For right now, just pretend I'm your date. It's fine."

I could see the worry in his eyes, though, even as he tried to make me feel better. I squeezed his hand.

It only took a matter of seconds to realize just how wrong he was.

We didn't have to look far to find Dr. Kelly. We'd barely set foot on the terrace when she appeared on the stage, microphone in hand.

"Good evening, everyone. If I could have your attention please."

The rooftop fell silent as fifty perfectly coiffed heads turned in her direction.

"I'd like to welcome you all tonight. This is a special evening indeed. Not only are we celebrating the three young ladies joining our ranks tonight, but we are also celebrating the return of one of our own." She held out a hand and instantly all those heads turned in our direction.

Izzy and I looked around, trying to figure out who the guest of honor was, but everyone was looking at us instead.

"What's going on?" I hissed at Izzy. "Why are they all looking at us?"

"I have no idea. Just smile like you know what's going on," Izzy replied.

"Oh, now don't be shy, ladies. Come on." Dr. Kelly waved us toward the stage. No one else moved. Izzy glided forward with me in her wake, gripping Micha's hand for dear life. I could feel his tension coming through every pore, through every synapse of my brain, and for once I knew I wasn't crazy to be scared. Something was horribly wrong with the entire setup. I tripped on the stupid high heels, stumbling slightly but managed not to fall.

Dr. Kelly took the mic from its stand and came to join us on the floor, just in front of the stage. The others formed a semicircle around us, their anticipation palpable.

"Isabella Cappelli. So good to see you again. You have the dubious honor of being the only candidate in the last thirty years to be put before the Sisterhood and then reject admission."

For a split second, Izzy looked gobsmacked, but she hid it under a thin veneer of *bitch, I will end you* politeness I'd only ever seen her pull out once, when my aunt Mary said something particularly offensive about her lifestyle over Christmas dinner.

Dr. Kelly, however, never lost her perky grin and barely skipped a beat as she turned to me. "And you, Genevra Cappelli. Returned to us at last, as you were meant to be."

There was a smattering of applause, but I could hardly hear it over the roaring in my ears.

Off to my left, I was aware of the crowd parting. Dressed in a dated, textured blue silk suit, the Dragon Lady eased her way through the audience, taking a front row seat to our humiliation. Micha took a step closer to me, pressing my shoulder into his chest protectively.

Dr. Kelly noticed her presence and gestured for her to come forward as well. "You know Sister Anaïs Traverse. Ladies, it is her that deserves the credit for discovering our lost daughter," she said, once again leading them in a polite round of applause.

The Dragon—Anaïs Traverse— appeared unfazed by the recognition. If anything, she only frowned deeper. She could have made scowling an Olympic event.

Izzy and I exchanged looks. She raised an eyebrow. *Is this true? Did you sign up for this?* the eyebrow asked. I shook my head.

Smooth as can be, Izzy stepped in to take Micha's place, looping her arm through mine. "Well, it was lovely to meet you all, but we must be going," she said, turning me around and making for the door.

"So soon? But we've barely even begun. And Genevra won't be going anywhere."

The women began to close ranks, cornering us by the stage. I held on to Izzy with one hand while Micha took my other.

Izzy was instantly on the defense. "What did you say?" she asked, all pretense of politeness gone. In an instant she was the hardened, scrappy troublemaker my grandmother always alluded to.

"I mean your presence isn't necessary for what we have in mind. You had your chance and you threw it away." Dr. Kelly matched my aunt glare for glare. She slipped the mic back into the holder, and the two women went toe to toe.

I didn't even notice two more of them coming up behind me until they'd grabbed my arms, pulling me back, and then everything happened at once.

Izzy whirled. "You let go of her right now!"

Kelly grabbed Izzy's arm. Izzy whipped around and decked her, laying her out flat on the hardwood.

The new members, marked by white Grecian robes, hemmed us in on one side while the others formed a circle, trapping us in place. Kelly, lip bleeding, sat up with fire in her eyes. Two more women went after Izzy, pinning her arms behind her back.

A black cloud began to form at Traverse's fingertips, drawing downward to the ground and bubbling up from the shadows around her.

As the sun sank lower, the last vestiges of daylight fading from the sky, two more shadows passed overhead.

The shadows surrounding Anaïs Travers began to take a shape, wriggling and writhing. Not a shape at all, really, but a mass. A swarm of hundreds of spiders.

At the sight of so many of the creepy bugs, I lost it. I screamed. Call me a wuss, but spiders freak me out more than almost anything else, and after the incident in the bathroom that phobia only got worse. When the roiling mass moved in our direction, I thought I would pass out. Izzy didn't see; she was too busy struggling against the women who held her—there were four of them now. She lashed out, kicking and using any dirty trick at hand, pulling hair and twisting strands of pearls into chokeholds. At some point, the delicate shawl tore off and lay trampled on the ground. Her heel caught on the fabric and she went down, taking two of them with her.

The shadow struck. Her two attackers, with their expensive dresses torn and hair ruined, leaped out of the way just in time.

I screamed Izzy's name as the swarm smothered her. Thin strands of spider silk whipped into the air, catching the breeze.

And then they were gone, melting into the dark

corners of the terrace, Izzy with them. Her figure simply vanished, like smoke into the night sky.

Screaming, crying, and now utterly alone and with no idea what to do, I sagged against the women holding me.

Dr. Kelly was back on her feet and in control of the scene.

With so many of them, I had no hope of escape. I stared at the floor, the tattered shawl, and the broken pin.

The stupid spider pin. Her stupid joke. What had she been thinking? I wanted to blame the entire thing on the pin.

"Evie!"

But I knew the truth. It was my fault. I'd gotten Izzy mixed up in this. I'd ignored her warning and that horrible feeling, and now it was too late.

Twinkle lights and red lanterns reflected off diamonds and sequins. Surrounded. No place to go. My bastion gone.

Images blended together in my brain, flashes of my vision in Dr. A's office combined with the scene on the terrace until I was no longer in Montreal, but back in the smoke filled temple, facing the soldiers.

Soldiers, with bronze medallions on their left shoulders. Medallions bearing the image of an owl.

The owl on the Athenian Society's logo.

I spotted it in half a dozen places: on a gold chain around someone's neck. Printed on the napkins, and airbrushed on the cake. Tattooed on Dr. Kelly's wrist.

I'd been hunted. Somehow, they'd been looking for me. Through a dozen incarnations, the followers of Athena had been sent for me—for Evadne—so long ago had morphed through the years to become a fucking sorority for psychos, somehow hunting me down and killed my aunt.

"Evie!"

I raised my head. Micha stood in front of me, trying to get my attention, to drag me out of my stupor. I looked past him at Dr. Kelly.

"Why? Why go through all of this? For me? I'm nothing."

"Your aunt gave you the book, didn't she?" Dr. Kelly asked, striding toward me. "I suspected as much when you entered my classroom. You see, many years ago, we thought she was the daughter of Arachne. She wasn't the first, but now she'll be the last. Our last mistake.

"She managed to get away. She turned down our offer, but by then we'd realized it couldn't be her. You see, the daughter of Arachne is one of Athena's most talented children. With her gifts, she could craft glorious things that could heal wounds. Protect the wearer. Even repair themselves. But she used them in the service of another goddess, giving her the credit for her skills. She not only rejected Athena and her followers, but placed a curse on them.

"She was supposed to be our sacrifice, to pay for the sins of her mother. She got away not once, but twice—the second time cheating us through her death. It has been our task since that time to find her." Dr. Kelly smiled wickedly. "For a time, we thought Isabella might be her. But no child of Athena would be able to give up her gifts as completely as she did once she chose to dedicate herself to another craft." She shrugged. "She was still talented, even if she wasn't the one we were looking for. We offered her a place among us, but she said no. Now, she has no choice but to be a part of our legion."

*Then she's still alive.* The thought made me struggle anew. "What did you do to her?"

Traverse stepped forward, and Dr. Kelly smiled.

"Sister Anaïs is one of our most talented members. She is the hiereia, the keeper of all we hold sacred. It is she who learned how to control Arachne and her vile offspring, and to use them to test potential candidates, to see if they were truly the daughters of Arachne." She smiled a little. "Saved us quite a lot of time. It was getting so tiresome having to explain what happened to the others, but we couldn't have them talking. They'd ruin our reputation with hysterical complaints. They're so much easier to manage when you can simply squash them like the bugs they are." As if on cue, she crushed one of the eight-legged monstrosities as it darted past her.

I gagged a little, but she didn't seem to notice.

"But now, we not only have you, we have your dear auntie as one of our legion, too." She was practically nose-to-nose with me as she held out a hand. A huge, hairy spider scampered up her tattooed wrist to rest in the palm of her hand, legs quivering as it fixed hundreds of eyes on me, its abdomen a brilliant scarlet. "I think it's only sweet revenge that she be the one to deliver the lethal blow. Arachne was the one who started this, and now it shall be family again who ends it. And with you dead, we shall have the perfect tribute—tribute to bring our goddess back into the mortal realm, where she belongs."

Eye to eye with that disgusting bug, I thought I was going to throw up. Had Izzy really been turned into a spider? This couldn't be happening. It wasn't. It just wasn't.

I met Micha's eye over Kelly's head. Formidable she might be, but tall she was not.

I swallowed a lump in my throat the size of a golf ball and looked back at the spider, then at Dr. Kelly.

If there was one thing I could say about the whole

bizarre evening, it was that I wasn't the crazy one in the room for once.

"Turn her back," I said, my voice trembling. "Turn her back right now."

Dr. Kelly laughed, glancing over her shoulder at Traverse like, *Will you get a load of this kid?* "No. I don't think I will. I like her much better this way. In fact, if you choose not to join us tonight, you might just end up joining her instead."

"Spending the rest of my life as a gag-inducing bug? I don't think so."

"Initiates, you know your places." Kelly stepped back to the stage.

The women in the circle bowed their heads as if in prayer. The initiates flanked me on either side, with one behind. They dragged me into the middle and I felt something sharp prodding me in the back.

Kelly raised her face skyward. When she looked back down at me she said: "Genevra Lucretia Maria Sophia Cappelli, in the name of the great goddess Athena, I grant thee one final decision: to dedicate thine life in the service of the goddess, or to sacrifice it to her glory. What is thy choice?"

I scanned the crowd, looking for anyone who seemed even remotely sympathetic. How could all of these women be riding on the same crazy train? At least one of them had to have a problem with *murder*.

My eyes darted to the two girls pinning me in place. "You're okay with this? You'd just let her kill me if I say no?"

The one on the right didn't flinch, but the one on the left shifted uncomfortably. She didn't take her eyes off Kelly. "Come on! If you guys are supposed to be pillars of the community, then you can't really think this is the right way to go about it!"

She didn't respond. I turned back to Kelly. "You're insane! And your recruitment program sucks!"

Eyes burning, she glared at me. "Choose!"

The girl on the left shifted again. "With respect madam, she's not even a postulate. How can she choose to dedicate herself when she doesn't even know—"

"Silence!"

"Forgive me, ma'am."

Kelly gave a jerk of her head. The crowd tore away the girl on the left, and the woman with the knife came forward to take her place. She gripped my bicep in her large hand, hard enough to bruise, and held the bronze dagger to my throat.

Kelly sneered down at me. "Choose."

My eyes locked with Micha's. "What do I do?" I asked. My mind was frozen. Yes or no, yes or no. Somehow, I thought joining this branch of Psychotics Anonymous might be worse than death, but what choice did I have?

Then again, maybe it would be better if I just didn't bother. Everything had turned into such a mess—how was I supposed to clean it up again?

"I'm going for help," Micha said suddenly. He vanished.

"No—"

"Prepare the sacrifice!"

What? "No, wait! That's not what I meant!" But my words were lost in the shuffle. The circled closed. The women in the front row, who were all dressed in red and white, knelt while the back row joined hands.

My captors released my arms. Momentarily stunned at being free, I didn't move. Kelly nodded at me. When I didn't move fast enough, the girls forced me down onto my knees until my forehead banged against the parquet dance floor.

Traverse opened her arms, eyes heavenward, and began chanting in what I assumed was Greek. Above us, the shadows I noticed earlier swooped down. An owl landed on each of her outstretched arms, glowing golden eyes fastened on me.

I cowered and looked around desperately, hoping for an escape.

Someone wheeled over a lit charcoal grill. The flames were three feet high and in them, I saw the temple from my nightmare. As Traverse's voice rose to a crescendo, the flames leapt even higher, taking on a sinister quality as the sky above began to fill with black clouds, blocking out the stars.

Traverse finished her invocation, and Kelly stepped up, head bowed, to take her place.

"Oh wise goddess, come to us in this place. We call you here, your servants, with an offering most pleasing, to bring you back into this realm from which you have so long been banished."

My eyes fell once again on Izzy's discarded shawl and welled with tears. My heart raced. Fear clogged my brain. There was no way out. What had I done? What could I do? This was all my fault. The mental voice I'd tried so hard to eradicate over the past few months was screaming, so loud that even if there had been an escape, I wouldn't have noticed it.

The shawl was nearby. Practically laying on the ground, I reached out a hand for it. The girls were too busy kneeling in rapture to notice. The gathering had gone from high-class party to tent revival, except instead of healing the sick they were planning to turn me into barbecue. Kelly's eyes had taken on the same ethereal glow as those of the owls; she was beyond the cares of the mortal world. Whatever she was doing, it seemed to be having an effect.

My fingers brushed the silk. Angora. A strand of Izzy's hair, caught in the fibers. Or was it mine? Long and black, it could be either. I dug my fingers into the stitches.

Why was I even fighting? A few months ago, dying had been my only wish. There was no point in continuing, and now I had no exit other than life as a spider or death.

I'd been fighting so hard for the last few months to get my life back on track. Had I been wasting my time? I clenched the lace in my fist.

No. Death might not bother me. But when it happened, it was going to be on *my* terms, not theirs.

When I looked back at the grill, there was a face forming in the flames.

No time like the present, then.

I threw the shawl. It hit Kelly full in the face. She stumbled, her words becoming incoherent as she tried to pull it off, but it clung there like a wet towel and wouldn't let go, tangling into her short hair and catching on the sequined collar of her dress.

In the split second distraction, I rolled away from the initiates and barreled through the women behind us, knocking them down by crashing my shoulder into their knees and hips. Packed in like sardines, if one went down, two more would follow.

I came up sprinting, diving for the elevator with them hot on my heels. I slammed my hand against the button, but the door didn't open. There was no way I'd be able to wait for it come up from the lobby, but there were no stairs I could see from this side of the café.

Miraculously, the shawl still held Kelly prisoner. The fabric formed a net covering her from head to toe. It stuck to her as if it was a real spider web.

I thought of my torn poncho, and the things Kelly had said about my former incarnation's powers.

I don't know how I did it, but I concentrated on the green and white awning overhead. Something popped, and then a lot of somethings. The heavy material collapsed, trapping half my pursuers in a makeshift net I barely avoided.

The elevator door dinged open behind me. I dove inside. As soon as the door shut, I ripped off my heels, leaving them abandoned in a corner of the elevator. When it reached the first floor, I bolted out the door barefoot, pushing through a crowd of shocked tourists. Everyone stared at me, and for once, I didn't care.

I ran straight into traffic; somehow I liked my chances better with a speeding bus than I did Kelly and her minions. Horns blared, but they only added to the noise pounding in my head. I was certain the owls were overhead, tracking my every move. I had to get off the street.

Places d'Armes Metro station. Without thinking I shoved the doors open and took the escalator two steps at a time down to the platform, hardly caring which direction the train was going.

They knew where I lived. They'd found me there before, and their creepy spiders—their legion—had been in the house.

The train pulled up as I careened onto the platform. I ran straight onto an empty car, skidding to a halt on the sticky floor and catching myself on one of the poles inside. Collapsing into one of the hard plastic seats, I covered my face, trying to catch my breath and figure out what to do.

"Micha."

The air beside me cooled noticeably, drawing goosebumps on my skin. He knelt in front of me and took my hand.

"What do I do?" I asked. My reserves were gone. My brain stopped working. My thoughts swirled in an endless circle of terrified nonsense.

"I need a safe place. But where can I go?"

The only other person I knew—that I trusted—in the city was Adam. I didn't want to put him in danger, but I didn't know where else to go.

I got off at my usual stop, but walked down to his building, just two streets over. One of the lights in the upstairs windows was still lit, and from the backyard I could hear what sounded like another party. I knocked on the front door. No one answered.

Peering around back, I saw I was right. Probably twenty people gathered in what appeared to be an impromptu end-of-the-year bash. Strings of lights hung from the trees. Beer bottles were all over, coolers open to the night air. I hid in shadow for several moments, watching, until I saw something move out of the corner of my eye. It was only a beetle, but for a second I thought it was a spider and nearly panicked.

Adam appeared on the back deck, beer in hand, peering at me over the railing. I saw him and nearly broke down.

"Evie! Are you all right? I thought—"

"I tried to come here, first, but he didn't understand me," Micha said.

"It's okay." I squeezed his hand.

Adam came down the steps and led me toward the back door. "Inside. Come on." He ushered me in without so much as a word to the partygoers.

"Come on. Up here." He pulled me into what I assumed was his bedroom. Closet sized, with posters from comic book movies on the walls, an old Mac desktop in the corner, and a TV propped up on milk crates housing DVDs and video game cases.

He sat me down on his bed. As soon as the door closed, I started to cry. I bawled. I don't know for how long. Adam knelt beside me and put his arms around me. I was shaking. When I could breathe enough to speak coherently again, I spilled out the story of the evening and how it had all gone terribly wrong. Adam stared at me, wide-eyed, in complete disbelief. He wouldn't have taken me seriously at all if not for his power.

"Don't worry," he said. "Just…don't worry for right now."

He lay me down, stroking my hair. "Just relax. It'll be fine. They won't find you here," he said.

I felt my muscles relax. My mind was still worried, but it was distant.

My eyes drooped.

He covered me with his blanket. "We'll talk in the morning. We'll get this figured out."

That was the last thing I remember.

# Chapter Nine
## I Miss My Train

It didn't occur to me until the next morning that he'd given me a magical roofie, using his empathy to somehow calm me down and put me to sleep when I otherwise would have been freaking out until dawn.

As it was, I woke up a little after seven, aware that, while I'd slept deeply, I'd paid for it with horrible nightmares. Still, they didn't compare to the one I'd lived through the night before.

In the morning light it felt distant, as though it had happened to someone else. Like I'd imagined the entire thing.

Micha sat in Adam's chair, legs crossed, leaning back against the desk and drumming his fingers against the pressboard with a grim look on his face.

I hadn't imagined it. It had been real.

I crawled out of bed and limped to the door on scraped feet. It was a miracle I hadn't stepped on a syringe or something during my barefoot run through the city. I knew my hair was a mess and it was obvious I'd slept in Izzy's dress. My breath tasted like something had died in the back of my mouth.

The house was quiet. I tiptoed down the hall, picking

my way through abandoned Solo cups, glass bottles, and empty pizza boxes. Dirty laundry hung on the banister. A couple slept on the floor between the coffee table and the television, and Adam had claimed the couch. He snored lightly, curly ponytail hanging over the armrest.

I crept up to him, but paused, not sure if I should wake him up to thank him, or just leave.

He solved the dilemma by cracking one eye open. He grunted, then rubbed his face, burying it into the throw pillow. When he looked up again, he looked a little less like the monster that lived under the bed and more like a very sleepy poodle with a static cling problem as his curls, loosed from the hair tie, flopped in strange directions or stood up on their own.

He gave a jaw-cracking yawn and sat up.

"Hey, sorry. I didn't mean to wake you. I just…I should probably go—"

Adam waved a dismissal through another yawn, shaking his head. "No. You're fine." Staggering to his feet, he looped an arm around my waist and led me back to the stairs. "Wait for me in my room. I'm going to make some coffee. You want some?"

"Um, sure?"

"Good. Then you can tell me what happened last night. A little more coherently. And we'll figure out what to do about it."

"Adam, no. Really. I'm sorry for crashing here, I just didn't know what else to do. You don't have to—"

"Yeah. I do. Don't worry about it. I got pulled into this already, so it's not your fault. Just hang on a second, okay? If I'm going to be dealing with goddesses and cults and all that—" he waved a hand suggestively, "then I really need caffeine first." He vanished into the kitchen. I sighed and went back up to his room. He joined me a few minutes later with two steaming mugs.

I clutched at mine, not really drinking it, as he asked me questions about the night before. When I repeated the part about Izzy turning into a spider, he paled noticeably.

"You're absolutely sure about all of this?" he asked when I was done.

I nodded. He downed the last of his coffee like it was a shot of something much stronger. "I don't know what to do," I said. "I don't know how I can get Izzy back, or get them to leave me alone. And it's not like I can go to the police and tell them they turned her into a spider. I'd get laughed out." With my history, I'd be lucky if they didn't lock me up for good, or charge me with her disappearance.

Shit. *What should I do?*

I took a deep breath. First thing, I needed shoes and a change of clothes, which meant going back to Izzy's. Maybe I'd get lucky and she'd be waiting for me in the living room, notes spread out on the floor, like nothing had happened. Maybe I'd get home and it would all have been a bad dream.

It sounded so good in my head that I set my mug on Adam's desk and stood.

"Where are you going?"

"Home."

"But you said they can find you there—"

"They can find me anywhere," I said, which was true. If Kelly and Traverse were using the owls and spiders to spy on me, then they could be anywhere. They probably already knew where I was. "But I need a shower and clean clothes, and I need to figure out my next move." And I needed my knitting. My fingers twitched from anxiety. I needed to do something productive with them before I went completely crazy. Having something in my hands helped me think.

"I'll walk you back," Adam said.

The house was still asleep, except for a little girl standing in the living room. She was about nine or ten, wearing a floral dress and bows in her hair.

"Why is there a kid here?" I asked, staring at her. She stared back and smiled.

"What are you talking about?"

I blinked, and she was gone.

The ghost. The one Micha mentioned in the graveyard. The one who liked to hide keys.

"Never mind." I rubbed the bridge of my nose. I could tell it was going to be a long day already.

Adam loaned me a pair of flip-flops, and left me at the front door. I promised to call him if I needed anything, and to do my best to stay out of trouble.

The flat was exactly as I'd left it: Izzy's things stacked by her chair, my knitting strewn on the couch. Her bedroom was empty except for the evidence of our emergency fashion crisis the night before, her good clothes rumpled on the bed where we'd discarded one item after another. I added the black dress to the pile. It was dirty and torn, but I didn't have the energy for a load of laundry or an attempt at repairs.

In my room, I found a tank top and a pair of jeans, trading out the fancy lace arm warmers for a simpler pair. I left Adam's sandals in a corner and grabbed my Converse. All the better for running in.

I took a long, hot shower, washing my hair twice and sobbing under the steam. I'd never felt so lost before. Things like this weren't supposed to happen. My entire life, I'd dreamed of finding magic the way the characters in my favorite books did, but now that it was here, it wasn't at all like I had hoped. I was finally starting to get

my life back on track, and then the rug got pulled out
from under me once again.

No matter what happened, I needed to figure it out
fast. How long would it be before someone noticed Izzy
was gone? What if one of my relatives called for her?
What would happen when the bills came?

"Stop it," I ordered myself. "Stop it. We aren't there
yet." I tried to remember Dr. Fisher's words. *Don't freak
out about things that haven't happened yet, and might not
happen at all. When things get out of hand, just
concentrate on the here and now. Tackle the things you
can control, and just take it one step at a time.*

Steadying myself, I got out of the shower and started
to get dressed. My reflection was sunken and tired
looking, with red-rimmed, hollow eyes and a scrape on
her cheek I didn't remember getting. To add insult to
injury, there was a zit on my chin that looked like it
might be a distant relative of The Mountain. You could
put a radio tower on the thing and get reception from
space.

"Great. Just great," I mumbled, dabbing some cream
on it. Downstairs, the doorbell rang. I wasn't even
wearing pants yet.

By the time I got downstairs, the delivery guy was
gone, but there were two packages on the front steps.

My birthday presents.

It just seemed cruel for all of this to happen on my
birthday. And then for my gifts to turn up late, too….

I brought them inside before I could fall apart again.

Mechanically, I got the scissors from the drawer in
the kitchen and used them to slice open the larger box
from my mom. Inside were razors, deodorant, and some
handmade soap with a designer label, along with a
wrapped package and a card. Mom hadn't added anything

to the printed message inside, which was very long and referenced at least three Bible passages. She'd signed for both her and Dad.

The present was a fancy makeup set. I stared at it for a moment, wondering when I was ever going to use it. The party the night before had been the first time I'd used cosmetics in probably a year, and look how that had ended. I tossed it back in the box, not sure if I should be offended everything she'd sent me had been personal hygiene products.

The smaller package had Izzy's name on it, but she'd told me to keep an eye out for a birthday present. And since my birthday was technically over, it couldn't hurt to open it, right?

I cut through the tape, peeling back the cardboard. Inside was a thin, print-on-demand paperback. More novella than novel, the front cover had a close up of a tattoo—a familiar tattoo. The orange and green snake was poised to strike, but its coiled tail was wrapped around a heart. The title read, "Adder's Breath," and listed Izzy as the author.

I stared at it in confusion for a moment. I knew all of Izzy's work; I did a lot of preliminary revisions for her and she always sent me copies of her books, even when I was living in Toronto, but I'd never heard of this one. And why had she used a picture of her tattoo for the cover?

Come to think of it, I'd never seen the whole thing before. It was on her chest, right above her heart. I'd only ever seen the snake's head, never the bottom part of the tail. I'd asked her about it once, but she just said it was personal, to remind her of something she'd done as a teenager she didn't want to forget.

There was no summary on the back. Inside, I found

the dedication:

*For my lovely Evie, so you will always know how much you are loved, even when I can't say the words out loud.*

Intrigued, I flipped to the first page and began to read.

***


I suppose the best way to put it is that the book was Izzy's autobiography. Written in her trademark style, it read like a work of fiction. At first, the story was familiar, describing a Christmas dinner when she came back to Toronto. I was seven. She described seeing me, hair in pigtails, red chenille holiday sweater, sitting quietly with a new book I'd been given while my cousins created chaos in the middle of my grandparents' living room with their new toys, all of which came with batteries and *without* earplugs.

She described me as her daughter.

In the flashback that followed, she was sixteen, sneaking out of the house after a fight with her parents. She'd been getting into bars for ages, and regularly passed for eighteen or twenty. Angry and sipping her drink, she was looking for trouble when a group of rookie cops walked in. She should have been scared, with her drink and her fake ID, but instead she was a little drunk and extremely reckless. She walked right up to the tallest one and started hitting on him. Fresh out of the academy, he'd come as part of an exchange program with several American police departments, and was more than eager to celebrate with an attractive, willing local.

They made love in the alley behind the bar, and when it was done he left her with two things: his name, Connor Adder; and me, though I didn't show up until a few months later.

When her family—my family—found out she was pregnant, they flipped. Told in no uncertain terms she would be giving the baby up, Izzy suffered through months of judgment and ridicule before finally giving birth. She didn't even get to hold me before the doctors took me away.

On my birth certificate, Izzy scrawled "unknown" for my father's name, and, under the stern gaze of her parents and siblings, she signed the adoption papers and agreed to never contradict the story that Paul and Margaret Cappelli, who could have no children of their own, were my parents.

Halfway through the book, I threw it down in disgust.

"Give it a chance," Micha said, picking it up off the rug and holding it out to me.

I stood. "Is that true? Did you know about this?" I demanded, my temper flaring with every word. "Did they really do that? Lie to me for my entire life?"

He hung his head. "It's not what you think."

"Oh, really? What is it then? Because it sounds an awful lot like my entire family—my parents, my grandparents, everyone—has been lying to me since the day I was born. And why?" I couldn't think of a reason. Was there ever a good reason to pull off a con that big on your own kid?

"They thought they were doing what was best. Izzy was different then. They thought she would be a bad influence."

Blood pounded in my ears. "A bad influence? She was a bad influence? Did you see what I grew up with?" My parents—or the people I'd always thought were my parents—weren't exactly the cuddly sort. There had been strict rules from day one. I had to blend in, be exactly like everyone else, but I also had to exceed every expectation. Perfect grades, athletic prowess, social grace. I'd failed on nearly every count, and no one let me forget it. Dad had hardly spoken to me since I'd tried to kill myself, and the one time he had all he did was yell—what a failure I was, making excuses, blaming others. I should have taken responsibility for my own actions. He accused me of being an attention seeker, and a coward. Months later, his words still made my eyes burn. Maybe I hadn't gone about things the right way, but what choice did I have at the time?

*Next time, I won't get caught.*

The thought came unbidden. I looked away. Micha reached for me, but I pushed him back.

"You know, I always kind of suspected they never wanted kids. But to get dumped on them? I almost feel bad for them. It's one thing when your loser kid is your own. But to get stuck with someone else's screw-up?" I laughed hollowly. "Suddenly, it all makes sense."

"Evie, no—"

"You said you've known me my entire life. Why didn't you tell me?"

"I…I couldn't. It was something you had to learn for yourself."

At least he had the sense to look ashamed.

"Right. You can tell me about goddesses and magic and past lives and things that aren't even supposed to exist, but you can't be bothered to tell me the person I've called Mother for my entire life isn't even related to me."

Micha bowed his head so low the silver forelock drooped down to obscure his face. Even without the psychic link binding us, I would have been able to sense his pain, but I didn't care. He was a liar and no better than the rest of my miserable family.

"Go away. Get out of my face. I never want to see you again," I ordered him, my voice so calm it scared even me.

"Evie, please—"

"Get out! I have enough liars in my life. The last thing I need is one hanging out in my head!"

He vanished, leaving me alone in the living room. For a moment, I stood there, panting as though I'd run a marathon. My eyes stung, but I was so angry even my tears seemed afraid to face me.

I swiped at my eyes with the back of my hand anyway. I needed to get out. I wanted to get the hell out of that flat, out of the city, but I didn't know where to go.

I started walking. I didn't know where I was going, and I didn't really care. I just needed to blow off some steam. I picked a generally northward direction, taking streets at random. My mood formed a thick cloud that hovered around me; other pedestrians gave me a wide berth on the sidewalk.

After a while—hours, maybe—my legs started to feel soft and weak. I kept walking until the jelly in my knees turned to burning knots in my thighs and calves.

I didn't know where I was. The neighborhood was one I'd never seen before. The houses were plainer, the yards smaller. It bore the distinct stamp of the housing boom of the 1950s, when cookie-cutter neighborhoods started springing up like weeds to meet demand. Interspersed with them were corner markets, tall apartment buildings, all of them bland, brick structures. Used clothing stores mixed with Doll-o-Rama and its competitors. The sidewalks were cracked and uneven, potholes in the streets. The stop sign at the end of the block listed to the right as though slightly drunk.

*Drunk sounds like a good idea.* A ways down, I saw

the logo for the Metro line. I didn't know which stop it was, but it hardly mattered.

My cell phone told me it was three o'clock in the afternoon. I'd been wandering for a good four hours, at least. My stomach rumbled.

From somewhere, I smelled onion rings. I started drooling like Pavlov's dog, following the scent across the road and over one street to a hole-in-the-wall place I could easily have walked past if I wasn't so hungry. Dimly lit and smelling of cigarette smoke, there was a wall of bottles behind the counter, and the entire menu, which consisted exclusively of fried foods, was written on a small blackboard.

I took a seat at the bar. There were only two other people in the tiny dining room. One of them appeared to be on his lunch break, and the other looked like the far end of the bar was his permanent address.

The bartender raised an eyebrow at me. I guess he didn't get many eighteen-year-old girls in at three pm, especially alone.

"Un rhum et coca, et un poutine, s'il vous plaît."

The barkeeper's other eyebrow went up, but he didn't comment. Didn't even ask for my ID.

He set the drink down in front of me. I downed half of it in one go.

I'm not a big drinker. I don't like alcohol much, usually sticking to wine coolers that don't taste much like adult beverages at all.

But every once in a while, it becomes necessary to drink with a purpose.

By the time my poutine came out, I was halfway through my second drink and the buzz was starting to break through my wall of anger. I took my food and retreated to a corner table where I could wallow without the watchful eye of the bartender pinning me down.

I felt like a white elephant gift, the one no one wants, but gets passed around from person to person, year after year, as a bad joke. Had any of them ever even wanted me? My mom, impatient, ever conscious of what others might think. "Don't sit that way, people will think you were raised in a barn." "Don't dress like that, you'll give the boys the wrong idea." "How are you going to explain that hair to your grandmother?" "Those aren't things we discuss. A real adult handles their own business, or do you want people to think you're incompetent?"

My dad, cold and distant. I got a hug once, maybe twice a year. The rest of the time I was lucky to get a grunt of acknowledgment, or a lecture on the poor decisions I made when he wasn't around to make them for me. My school, my extracurricular activities, they all had to meet his standards, as if he was trying to prove something. In retrospect, I guess he was.

They were afraid Izzy would be a bad influence. I had to be better. I had to prove to them—to everyone—that I wasn't my mother. That I was better than Izzy. My entire life, they'd been holding me against a specific set of standards I hadn't even known about. Better grades in math and science, check. Better manners, check. No disciplinary action at school, check. Not pregnant at sixteen, check!

And what about Izzy? Had she really wanted me to come back? I remembered when I was little, how aloof she always was at family gatherings. I hadn't understood at the time, but now I knew—they were watching her. Making sure she didn't get too close to me, to exert her "bad influence."

I finished my drink and ordered another. The gravy on my poutine was getting cold, turning into a congealed mess of grease and flavoring. I poked at it with one of my fries. They were the kind found in the freezer section of the local market, not the awesome homemade, gushy kind that were so perfect for the dish. As they inched closer to room temperature, they got stiffer and crunchier. Ew.

When my third rum and Coke arrived, I decided I was, in fact, drunk. Probably drunker than I should have been. I sipped it, and tried to remember the last time I'd had more than a wine cooler.

Right. The graduation party. I'd gone with my friend Alice to a party someone from school was throwing. One of my many failings was that I was not and never would be a social butterfly. Alice joined a group in the living room, while I found myself alone on the back deck, watching a dozen people I'd gone to school with for years but had never once spoken to, talk and laugh and toss each other in the pool. With no one to talk to and no way home, I was stuck. The first beer loosened me up. The second had me talking to the cute boy in the hockey jersey I'd been eyeing for two weeks but whose name I didn't know. By the third I'd forgotten his name, and halfway through the fourth I was hiding in the backseat of Alice's Bug, crying myself to sleep over what an incompetent moron I was.

And I spent the whole of the next morning praying to the porcelain god while my mom had a panic attack in the hallway and kept asking if I was pregnant and if I'd been careful. At the time, it had been annoying and hadn't really made sense, and I'd been more concerned with the fact that my insides were on my outside and my head was trying to explode, but now it made perfect sense.

Once again, I hadn't lived up to the invisible standard no one told me about.

Disgusted with everything, I threw my money down

on the table and left.

***

It took a while, but I found my way back to the Metro station. I was way up near the northern end of the orange line. I collapsed onto a seat, completely oblivious of everyone and everything around me. I knew the smart thing to do after three rum and Cokes—or was it four?—was to take my lightweight self home and sleep it off, rather than wandering the streets. I knew this, and yet I couldn't face the idea of going back to Izzy's. What would I do? Sit around and watch television while the psycho sorority sisters held my aunt prisoner? Should I go after them, and risk joining her? How could I even find them? What would I do once I did? And a better question: why hadn't they come for me?

Because they already knew where to find me, at any time, I realized, watching a spider scuttle across the floor of the car. I thought about stepping on it, just in case it was part of the Legion. But then, I remembered what Kelly had said: every one of those spiders represented a failed attempt to find me, or one of my other incarnations. Every one of them was once a person.

I paused, drawing my foot back. The spider didn't even slow down, oblivious to how close it came to being another greasy smear on the floor of a subway car.

*I hope no one steps on Izzy*, I thought.

Well, that was new. You know your life has gotten weird when your fondest wish is that no one steps on your aunt.

Mother.

Mom?

*Izzy*. For the moment, it was just easier.

The train rocked me like a cradle, lulling me into a sleepy, unfocused state. I watched the stations flash by without seeing them, my window blinking from darkness to light.

The car was hot, air conditioning barely functioning. Sweat beaded on my neck. I laid my head against the cool window and closed my eyes. Over and over again, the mantra, "My fault. All my fault," replayed in time with the *schuck-schuck* sound of the tracks. When we reached Jean-Tallon Station, I should have gotten off and switched to the blue line, but I just sat there, exhaustion gluing me to the seat. The car filled with people on their evening commute. I squished myself closer to the wall, eyes closed, head down, avoiding them all. As we pulled out of the station, the train announced my shortcomings to the other passengers. *My fault, my fault. All my fault.*

The wave of hopelessness crashed over me. Tears pricked behind my eyes. I sat through Berri-UQAM, the main terminal, and didn't move as the train lurched through Place d'Armes and continued its journey south to Lionel-Groulx.

As we entered the last leg of the orange line, the train's insults became more varied: *stupid, worthless, unwanted. What could you do?*

Finally, at Snowden, I got off. I could take the blue line two stops to Edward-Monpetite, or I could just walk.

I needed time before I could face Izzy's apartment. I left the station, quickly abandoning the busy street for quieter residential ones.

There were still a few hours of daylight left, but darkness surrounded me, engulfed me.

There was no way out. I knew this feeling. It was the same one I'd fought against for so long, before finally giving in.

I took the pills, just like I was supposed to. I didn't
want to. Most of the time, they made me feel so sick I
could hardly eat. I'd gone through bouts where I didn't
sleep for days, and then slept for sixteen or twenty hours
straight. Dr. Archambault said my dosage needed
tweaking, that we'd see how I did on my current
prescription before trying another. He liked to give it at
least two months to see how things went, wait for my
hormones to get back into balance.

I would say I wasn't doing well at all.

I wondered, idly, how long I would have to take those
pills. Compressed chemicals, poison, that didn't really
work all that well. The list of side effects was as long as
my arm. Some days, I preferred dealing with the
depression over the medication. But either way, I was
still going to be defective for the rest of my life, fighting
the darkest reaches of my mind every time I got up in the
morning, and every night as I lay awake in bed, trying to
find enough peace to sleep.

*So this is it.* The past few days of feeling almost
normal—that was as good as I was ever going to get.

Normal people went to school, dated, got married. I
got passed from one family member to another like a hot
potato, hunted down by my shrink's secretary, and my
aunt turned into a spider.

My feet carried me past the University of Montreal.
Once I crossed the train tracks, I'd be in Izzy's
neighborhood.

From a distance came the sound of the whistle, one of
the evening commuter trains that crisscrossed Quebec
and Ontario, perhaps, or a freight train.

Gravel crunched under my feet. I balanced briefly on
the rail, then stepped down onto one of the thick wooden
ties. Mixed in with the white and grey gravel was the

detritus of city life: a Coke can, a broken beer bottle. Someone had tried to flatten a penny, but placed it wrong. It sat on the tie, remarkably undisturbed by the vibrations.

The train was now a rumble I could feel in the soles of my feet. I crouched down to inspect something glittering in the crushed limestone.

Mica.

Micha.

"Evie…"

"I told you to go away," I said.

"You really are crazy if you think I'm just going to stand here and—" He reached for me, but with an outstretched hand I pushed him away. I was getting good at it.

"Leave me alone." It was better that way. It really was. Eventually, he'd come to understand. Everyone was better off without me.

"You don't really believe that. What about Izzy? If you don't help her, who will? And Mike. He found you last time. Who will it be this time? You promised you wouldn't do that to him again. And your mom—"

"Don't talk to me about her," I growled. "I don't want to hear it. She is not my mother. She lied to me for my entire life. Why would I even care what she thinks?"

The whistle blew again, much closer this time. I had to shout to make myself heard. "I will not—"

Another whistle. I turned. I was practically face to face with the train—

And then I wasn't. I was flat on the ground with no air in my lungs, and something heavy on top of me.

"That wasn't your smartest move, there," said my rescuer, sitting up.

I sucked in a much needed breath. My hands bled from scrapes dotted with gravel and I was pretty sure I had at least one or two bruises, but I was fine. "What the hell? What were you…" My words trailed off when he stood up. Even from the ground, I could tell he was easily the tallest man I'd ever seen.

Somewhere in his thirties, he had bright red hair. His three-piece pinstriped suit looked like it cost as much as a year at university, even with the limestone dust clinging to the wool. He stooped to retrieve his fedora from the gravel where it lay near his wing-tipped shoes.

"Who are you?" It didn't come out as angry as I'd hoped. My voice trembled a little bit, intimidated by his oversized shadow.

"Ian. Ian Mulhaney."

I scrambled to my feet. Whoever this guy was, he didn't look like the type to go rolling around in the dirt by choice. He brushed the dust from his suit, the creases falling perfectly back into place. A tiny pin on his lapel glinted. There was a star, but I couldn't get a good look at it when he was moving.

Micha came to stand beside me. He reached for my hand and I let him. There was something about Mr. Mulhaney and his incredibly blue, blue eyes that frightened me. Not in the same way crazy Dr. Kelly had. This was a deeper instinct, something much more primal. There was something behind the calm gaze that brooked no argument—whatever this man told you to do, you did.

"I, um. Thanks."

Mulhaney looked down his nose at me. "Don't lie just to save face. We both know you're far from grateful."

I couldn't have been more shocked if he'd slapped me. Though my own response came close. "Sorry. Canadian. Force of habit."

Satisfied the suit would survive, he dropped his hands, hooking them into his pockets. "Well, you'll get over it soon enough, I'd imagine."

"What's that supposed to mean?"

"You've got a rough road ahead, kid. And you're not going to get very far on it if you keep making up excuses and ignoring what's right in your face. Like that one there." He nodded at Micha. "I can't believe anyone would buy into that spirit bullshit, especially you. You've been around long even to know the difference, haven't you?"

Micha just looked confused.

Mulhaney rolled his eyes. "Kid, you're no more spirit than I am. You're a ghost. Dead. Anyone with any Sight at all could tell you that. Do you think your empath friend would be able to sense a spirit? Have you ever seen one?" he asked me.

I shook my head. "I don't think so."

"See? Ghost. Hate to break it to ya, pal, but you're dead. You have been for a while." He pulled a silver cigarette case out of his pocket as he turned away.

"Wait. Who are you? What were you doing here?"

"Just keeping an eye on you, kid," he said around the cigarette as he lit up. "I've got a feeling you're going to be very important later on, and I want to make sure you live to see it."

His eyes softened, just a little. He put a hand on my head like I was a little kid. I kind of felt like one, since I barely even reached his shoulder. "You remind me of one of my grandkids, you know that? He was in a spot a lot like yours a while back. But don't worry. If that idiot can make it through, then so can you. You've got the Adder pluck, if you'll let it come out once in a while."

*Adder.* There was that name again. "How do you…how do you know my father?"

"Kid…Evie…I've known about you for a long time.

We keep track of our own, but we can't always interfere."

Gee, where had I heard *that* one before? I felt my anger rising up again. I tore myself away from the condescending hand on my scalp. "You know what? I'm getting sick and fucking tired of everyone watching out for me, but never doing a damn thing to help. You say you take care of your own, well where were you last year? Where were you when I was a scared little kid, hiding in the closet? Where were you when my grandparents took me away from my mother and gave me to my mom and dad? I don't need your kind of help, thanks. I'm doing just fine on my own."

He smiled, just a little. "There, see? I told you. Pluck. You better hang on to that. You'll be needing it." He waved a little with the hand holding the cigarette, smoke wrapping around his fingers like silver rings. With his other, he pulled a business card from his breast pocket.

I took it. It was plain cream paper, thick and fancy—not some cheap overnight printing job. In sepia ink, embossed letters read: Ian Mulhaney. There was a phone number with an American area code underneath. Off to the side was a logo. A nine-pointed star, the same as his lapel pin.

"If you ever need any help, just give me a shout. And if you're ever in Chicago, you should look me up. I know a couple of boys who'd love to meet you."

"You know what, keep your card. I really don't need to be set up by some creepy stranger." I flipped it back at him and stalked off. When I glanced back at the end of the block, he was gone.

His words played back at me. "I've got some boys who'd love to meet you," I mocked. "We look out for our own. Look me up if you're ever in Chicago."

I was halfway across Mount Royal Boulevard when it

hit me.

"Did he say grandchildren?"

# Chapter Ten
# Roll for Initiative

I went home and drank myself to sleep so I wouldn't have to pay attention to how empty the apartment felt. My anger dissipated, leaving me with the same exhausted hopelessness as before. I fell asleep fully clothed, and woke up ten hours later still lying on top of my blankets. I got up long enough to take off my shoes and jeans, then crawled back under the covers, pulling them up to block the light coming through my open windows.

Outside, birds chirped and the fresh scent of a multitude of flowering trees came in on the light breeze. It was warm and pleasant without being hot; the humidity hadn't reached its peak yet.

But moving was too much. I just wanted to lie there with my eyes closed. There was no reason to get up. No one was waiting for me.

I dozed on and off through the morning, but couldn't bring myself to get out of bed.

Here's the thing about depression—if the disease itself doesn't suck all of the life and energy out of you, then the medication will. And sometimes, you don't know why you're upset or hopeless or scared or worried—you

just are, and it overtakes everything. The darkness
consumes every thought, every feeling, until there's no
room for any other emotion. It warps your perception of
the world and yourself until you become pinned to the
bottom of an endless black pit, and sunshine and
happiness aren't just distant memories—they're
something you're not even entitled to, something meant
for other people. Anyone but you.

The hangover from hell didn't help.

"Okay, enough of this," Micha said suddenly.

The blankets flew off and landed on the floor.

"Hey!" I pulled my knees up to my chest. After the
cozy warmth of my bed, the room was freezing.

"Get up. You need to get out. You need a distraction.
If you get the blood flowing, then your brain will follow
and we'll be able to find a way out of this mess."

"Did you miss yesterday, when I was walking all over
creation? If that didn't get the blood flowing, I don't know
what will. Now go away. I told you I don't want to see
you anymore." My legs and back still hurt from walking.
My head throbbed from the hangover, and there was a
good chance that if I moved I'd be sick. I covered my
head with the pillow and wished I was dead.

The pillow took flight.

"Izzy is depending on you, Evie," Micha said, bracing
his hands on the mattress to look me eye to eye. "Are you
going to let her down?"

"What can I do? I'm just a stupid girl." *The one who
got her into this mess in the first place.*

"That is what we need to figure out." He grabbed my
wrist, dragging me into a sitting position. "Get dressed.
Put on some shoes. No, take a shower first. You need
one." He touched my hair, which had gone stringy and
gross from the hike the day before.

I batted his hand away and smoothed it down self-consciously. I did kind of stink a little. But what did it really matter? It wasn't like—

"Oh, no you don't," he said, grabbing my shoulders when I tried to lie down again. "First things first. Shower. Change clothes. Put a load of laundry in while you're at it. You're almost out of underwear."

"What would you know about that?"

He avoided the question. "And get your knitting bag together. I want to try something. We're going to see just what you're capable of."

***

Call him a ghost, or a spirit, or whatever you like. I just called Micha annoying. He wouldn't let me go back to bed and made a royal pain of himself until I got in the shower. I made him wait in the hall, since he'd apparently been inspecting my underwear drawer. Who knew what else the peeping ghost was up to?

I had to delve into the far reaches of my closet to find something marginally clean: a black and gray rugby shirt, my last pair of jeans, and combat boots. I finished the look off with some thick leather cuffs I'd bought from the market at the Tam-Tams on Sunday morning. With two thick wooden needles poking out of my messenger bag and my hair pulled back in a ponytail covered by a black bandana, I was ready.

"Okay. So where are we going?"

"You've lost track of the days again, haven't you?" he said as I dragged myself down the stairs to the front door.

No point arguing, since it wasn't really a question. My internal calendar usually came down to "days I work" and "days I don't work," with little difference between the two except the latter may or may not involve pants. "So what?"

"It's Sunday. And it's about noon."

"Still not seeing the point."

"Walk with me."

I rolled my eyes but I didn't have much choice. Limbs heavy, I followed him down Côte-Sainte-Catherine until we reached the intersection with Voie Camillien Houde, grateful for my thick sunglasses. Summers might be short in Canada, but they can be intense. Sweat rolled down the back of my neck before we got to the end of the street.

Mount Royal Park was packed. There were half a dozen games of Frisbee going, and picnics spread out all over the side of the Mountain. While I waited for the crosswalk signal to change, the DJ tapped his mic, testing the PA system before launching into a French welcome that I couldn't make out over the sounds of traffic. Shortly thereafter, music began pulsing through the air.

Tam-Tams is probably my favorite thing in the entire city. May through September, rain or shine, you'll find people out on Sunday afternoons gathering for the drum circle.

I don't know what started the tradition, but since it's rooted in the '70s, I'm assuming hippies were involved. It seems like the whole city comes out with their drums to dance barefoot on the grass. Some of them dance to the DJ, others form their own drum circles with guitars, violins, flutes, or other instruments joining in. Sometimes there are professional belly dancers, and other times it's just couples out to have some fun, or members of the audience who enjoy a good beat.

Kids played catch with their dads and fetch with their dogs. Local artisans laid out blankets to display their wares, everything from tooled leather—like my cuffs—to paintings, woodcarvings, anything imaginable.

"You could sell something here," Micha whispered in my ear, his hand gliding over my lower back. "You make some amazing things; I'm sure people would love to buy your accessories, or your yarn. You should get out your spinning wheel again."

"Shut up. I'm still mad at you," I hissed through clenched teeth. I nodded when one of the vendors looked up at me. Most were still setting up their spaces; it was a little early for them.

Farther up the hill, past the athletic displays, there were sunbathers, then the drum circles—mostly sheltered in the shade at the edge of the woods. Since it was Montreal, a good chunk of them were smoking. Since it was Tam-Tams, a good chunk of them weren't smoking tobacco.

I started to take a seat under one of the trees, pressing my back to the bark and hugging my bag. The space was too open. Exposed. I wanted to go back home.

"Come on. This way." Micha took my hand, pulling me toward the LARPing area.

The Live Action Role Play area was a big rectangle, stomped down so fiercely nothing could grow there. Sometimes the crowds were huge. I'd seen upward of a hundred people on the field going at each other in complete melee style with foam weapons, but there were only about fifteen when I arrived.

"What are we doing here? They haven't even started yet."

"You're going to play."

"What?"

"Just go up. Ask if you can borrow a sword from someone."

"I am not just going to dive in there! I don't know the

rules, or how it's done."

"It's a sword. Pointy end goes in the other guy."

"It's fake. It's not going into anyone."

I caught one of the guys setting up looking at me, and remembered that, with few exceptions, I was the only one who could see Micha.

Great. Not only did I get to ask a stranger if I could borrow his toy sword, but I had to do it as the crazy girl who talked to herself.

It got even more awkward when the guy wrangling the weapons only spoke French, and very fast. I discovered, even after twelve years of French, my vocabulary still didn't cover things like swords and gaming. Through a combination of disjointed French, English, and a little mime, I managed to get the point across and walked away with a foam and duct tape broadsword reinforced with a dowel rod.

*Okay, now what?* I wondered, standing at the edge of the field, watching four guys pummel each other with fake swords and a battle ax. One of them was wearing a *Doctor Who* T-shirt and a cape. His opponent looked like he'd just left a Marilyn Manson concert. There was more metal on his person than in the average motor vehicle.

Movement out of the corner of my eye. The keeper of the swords rushed at me, swinging his weapon up with a feral battle cry. He stopped short of hitting me by about two feet, raising an eyebrow when I automatically covered my face and ducked.

I held up my sword with one hand. "En garde?"

He laughed. He held up his sword, showing how he gripped it. "*Deux mains*," he explained. "Ce n'est pas un fleuret."

Right. Big sword. Not a fencing foil. I grabbed the hilt with both hands, a bit like a baseball bat. My teacher smiled and nodded, and then came at me again, a little slower this time. Still in French, he gave me a rundown of the rules. "You can't hit anyone in the head, neck, or groin. Those are illegal. If you get hit on a limb," he tapped my shoulder lightly with his sword, "then you are injured and have to hold it behind your back. Since you're not wearing armor, torso shots mean you are dead." He demonstrated the pose that meant "dead": crouched with his sword held behind his neck. "But we don't really do that here, so you can either step out and let someone else use your weapon, or take a break for a couple of minutes and then keep going. It's sort of continuous."

I nodded. When he was back on his feet, I jabbed at him and missed. He swung down and knocked my sword out of my hands. It went flying to the other end of the field.

I ran to retrieve it while he laughed. My face got red. *I knew this was a bad idea. I'm making an idiot of myself.*

"Hey, ce n'est pas grand-chose," he said when he saw my expression.

I forced a smile and tried to rein in my nerves. I was so keyed up, I was liable to start crying at any second. Or just run away. Running sounded like a good idea, but Micha glared at me from the sidelines and I went back to my place.

"Je m'appelle Vince. Vous?"

"Eh, Evie," I said. Trying to concentrate on French and swordplay at the same time wasn't easy. Within three moves, Vince had me disarmed again. On our third round, he got my left arm when I tried to block him. With only one usable hand, it wasn't long before he'd "cut off" all of my other limbs, too, and I was effectively dead.

"Break now, no?"

"Yes. A break." I got off the field before I could do

anything else stupid.

The battleground was filling up fast as the afternoon got into full swing. Music pulsed from all over, a mix of rock, reggae, and tribal with bits of other genres thrown in. At least thirty people were now battling it out with their makeshift weapons. Near the center of the fray was an undersized kid dressed in a brown faux fur barbarian costume, with a war hammer as tall as he was and enormous foam platforms attached to his shoes, turning him into a giant. He let out a roar and brought the hammer down on a man twice his age in full samurai armor. A blond girl in elf ears and a chain mail bikini top backed up the samurai.

I sat down on the grass, retrieving my messenger bag. Others had piled up their belongings nearby, and a young mother with a pair of toddlers kept a lax guard over them while they watched Daddy play.

I'd been smart enough to stick a bottle of water in my bag before I left that morning, and I was incredibly grateful for it now. The battle kicked up tons of dust; I already needed another shower.

Without me to coach, Vince joined the fight in earnest, tackling what looked like a vampire and a tall, skinny guy in a plaid shirt and torn jeans.

"That wasn't bad," Micha said, sitting beside me.

"That was terrible."

"You'll get the hang of it."

"Remind me again why you're forcing me to do this?"

"Shall I list the reasons?"

"Please do."

I'd only been sarcastic, but Micha decided to take me seriously.

"One, you need to get out of the house. Two, you need social interaction. Three, you need physical activity.

Four, this will play into your self-defense training—"

"Wait, what?"

"You're going to need it."

Well, couldn't argue there….

He continued: "Plus, if you're going up against servants of Athena, then you'll probably need to know how to use a sword at some point."

"I doubt this is actually going to help me, then. Considering kill shots are illegal and you're not supposed to go around whacking people at full strength."

"Maybe not, but I didn't think I could convince you to pay for fencing lessons, and in class you'll always be fighting one on one, with set styles and rules. This is…a little more chaotic. You'll learn to think better on your feet. Which you suck at, by the way."

"I also suck at thinking on my ass, but I don't see that changing anytime soon." Frustrated, I delved into my bag and pulled out my project, an openwork market bag. There were already about a dozen of them in the pantry back home, but it was a good, mindless project and that was what I needed, since my brain kept panicking and running off in every conceivable direction except the one it should be going in.

"It needs work, sure, but you can do it. I've seen the things you can do. When you're in your element, you're a total badass."

I snorted.

I could feel Micha's frustration growing. It was about damn time. The guy was way too patient with me. It was like he wasn't even human. Okay, so technically, as a ghost, he wasn't human, but at one point he was. Anyway, no one is that much of a saint. Everyone got sick of my damage at some point. They all had their limits.

After nine months, it was about time I found his.

"Do you remember the vision you had, in the doctor's office?" he asked suddenly.

"What? Well, yeah." The one with Micha's head getting cut off. And me dying. Yeah, I remembered it pretty vividly. It had featured prominently in the nightmares I'd been having—at least, the ones that didn't involve Izzy, spiders and rabid owls.

"At the very beginning, you saw yourself. You were kicking butt and taking names."

"That was…different. It wasn't me. It was…someone else."

"Her name was Evadne. And you were her, once upon a time. It was a memory, Evie. A memory of who you once were. Who you have the potential to be now."

The woman with the kids was starting to notice me talking to myself. I shoved my knitting in my bag and made for the woods. The trails might be a little less crowded; with luck, my spot by the rocks would be empty. I was done with people for the day.

"Evie, you have to go back. You need to train some more—"

"It's not training, and I have reached my quota for social interaction," I said from behind clenched teeth. A passing jogger gave me a sidelong look. I sighed and peeled off to take n overgrown side path. "Besides, I'm still mad at you."

"If you don't stop and listen to me, then I won't leave you alone," he threatened childishly.

"Right. You know, for being a couple hundred years old, you sure are immature," I snapped.

Micha fumed. I grabbed onto a low hanging limb, using it to pull myself up a steep, unmarked incline, a shortcut to my spot.

"Why are you fighting me? I'm trying to help you. I'm not going anywhere. You can't drive me away by acting like a brat."

I couldn't even find the words, I was so angry with him. "What even gives you the right to show up like this and ruin my life?" I demanded. "I was just fine before you showed up. I could have gotten better like a normal person, but instead I always have you hanging around. If I'd told the doctors I could see you, they would have doped me up so bad I never would have gotten out of there. And now you keep hanging around, making your stupid comments, and trying to run my life—"

"I'm not trying to run your life! I'm trying to make sure you have a life to ruin!"

"What's it even matter to you? You're dead. Don't you have pearly gates to go through or something? Hanging out for how long now? Get an afterlife already!"

"I'm here because I love you!"

The declaration seemed to take all of the wind out of his sails. His head dropped and he leaned back against one of the boulders. "I love you, okay? I might not remember when we were together, but I've been in love with you from the moment I made it my mission to protect you."

"Well you're doing a bang-up job of it."

It was a cruel thing to say and I knew it, but it came out anyway. Micha continued to stare at the ground, shoulders slumped.

"I don't have anywhere else to go," he said finally. "I can't move on, even if I wanted to. I've seen ghosts. I've seen spirits. Ghosts fade after a while. They move on. They lose who they are and either become nothing more than a collection of malevolent energy, or they vanish altogether. Spirits can't feel. They attach themselves to a person or a place, and it becomes their purpose. The only reason they exist is to keep what they hold dear safe.

"So maybe that guy was right, and I am a ghost. But if I am, I've been bound to this plane until I can get things right. I can't leave unless I know you are safe, and that's not going to happen unless you get your act together and start trying to meet me halfway."

Right. Now we were back to everything being my fault again.

When he looked up at me, his gray eyes brimmed with hurt and anger. "For centuries, you have been my entire reason for being. My purpose for existing. Maybe you don't understand what that means, to dedicate your entire self to another person and their survival, but it's what I chose to do. But maybe you're right. I can't fix you. I can't save you. I should have realized that by now."

I opened my mouth to protest, but he was gone.

***

By the time I got home from the park, my mood was even more sour than it had been that morning. The last thing I wanted was to talk to anyone, especially if we were related to me, but I had eight missed calls on my cell phone, and I couldn't keep rejecting calls indefinitely.

No matter how much I wanted to.

*I do not have the energy for this*, I thought, punching the green button on my cell. "Hello?"

"Hey, Ginny-bug! How's the birthday girl?" Uncle Mike asked. Despite everything, I still felt myself warm at the sound of his voice. Uncle Mike has been one of my favorite people in the entire world since I was old enough to crawl. I heaved an internal sigh of relief that it wasn't one of my parents.

"My birthday was two days ago," I said, but I was smiling, just a little.

"Eh, what's a couple of days? I tried calling then, but you didn't answer. You guys must have had one hell of a party," he joked, knowing full-well the likelihood of Izzy and I throwing a wild party was about as likely as my family deciding to forgive everything and stop hassling the two of us.

"Yeah, sorry. I've been busy the last couple of days."

"How's Izzy? I haven't been able to reach her, either."

"Yeah. Um. She's fine. She just…her phone died. She hasn't gone in to get a new one." It was a weak lie at best. Izzy was almost as attached to her phone as she was to her laptop. The woman was a complete Twitter addict.

"Oh, that's too bad."

I couldn't tell if I heard confusion or suspicion in his voice. I swallowed a tightness in my throat. Mike was kind, the family mediator. He'd kept the tenuous peace between Izzy and the rest of the family, and he'd been my advocate when I was…sick. But he was also a homicide detective.

We chatted a little while longer. I tried to steer the conversation away from Izzy. I told him she was out. He asked what we'd done for my birthday, and I told him we went to a party.

"Your mom told me something about that… Have you talked to her lately?"

Great. Here it was. "No. Not since she called for my birthday."

"She told me the two of you got into an argument." When I didn't answer, he continued. "Are you okay, Ginny-bug? Is there something I can do?"

"No. I think everyone has done enough."

I didn't mean for it to come out so sharp. I didn't mean

for it to come out at all. Words appeared to be my enemy.

"What do you mean?"

I closed my eyes. I knew it would be better to handle things calmly, not lash out at one of the few people who really cared about me.

But he knew, I reminded myself. He knew, and he never said anything. Just like all of them. He kept the secret.

"Nothing." The anger bubbled under the surface, but I held it in check, barely. I couldn't keep it from grinding in my voice like broken glass on pavement, but I at least kept my words from oozing bile. I knew if I tried to talk about it, then the whole thing would explode.

"Evie?"

"I just don't want to talk to anyone right now. Especially my parents."

Mike was quiet for so long I considered hanging up. "She told you, didn't she? Izzy, I mean. She told you what happened when you were born."

The bile decided to overflow from my eyes. "They lied to me, Uncle Mike. They lied to me for my entire life. Everyone did. Even you."

Mike always pinched the bridge of his nose when he got stressed. I could picture him doing it then.

"It wasn't my secret to tell, honey," he said at last. "I disagreed with it. I tried to talk my parents out of it, and I tried to tell Paul he should tell you, but they wouldn't do it. They were all too afraid. They thought it was best when you were a kid, if you didn't know. That it would make things less confusing for you. And when you got older, they just wanted what was best for you. You were having such a hard time… And the longer they kept the secret, the easier it was for them to believe it was true."

"You could have told me." There. A blatant

accusation. They all could have told me, at any time. Even Izzy. But none of them ever did.

"It wasn't my secret. You're not my daughter."

"Well it looks like you're the only one who feels that way."

I ended the call before I could say anything else horrible. It rang in my hand, so I turned it off.

I'd had enough talking for one day.

The apartment was too empty. I bounced around the rooms for a while like one of those old-fashioned games with the mazes and the ball bearings, but I had no direction, and no purpose. Story of my life.

I took my knitting and started walking. Parc Outremont.

Sitting next to the monument, I jammed my needles into my project. If knitting could be violent, I managed it.

"Who needs them, anyway? Assholes. Jerks. What did they think they were doing? That it would be okay to just not tell me anything for eighteen years, and then hope it turned out all right?"

I jabbed the needle in for another stitch, wrapping the yarn in a chokehold around the tip before pulling it back through.

"Is that for the war effort?"

I looked up, startled.

It was the soldier again. I felt a chill go up my spine. Should I mention the fact that he was a ghost? How do you talk to the dead?

He was still waiting for an answer. "I—no. This is just…it's for myself," I said hastily. Nerves made me knit faster.

"You haven't seen Anna, have you?"

"No. No, I haven't. Still haven't found her?"

He shook his head sadly. "I've been waiting for so

long. I thought she would be here by now."

"How long have you been waiting?"

He sat down beside me, tilting his head back as he thought. "I'm not sure. But a very long time. We were supposed to go to the pictures, you see. But I think the show must be over by now."

I looked at his wool uniform, the stripes sewn to the shoulders, and his neat little cap, perched on greased hair. Yeah, that show was long over. "It was Etienne, wasn't it?"

"Yes. Lieutenant Etienne Passard." He held out his hand to shake, a big grin on his face like there was nothing that brightened his day more than meeting strangers in a park. "I don't think I got your name last time."

"Evie. Evie Cappelli."

"Are you waiting for someone, too?" he asked, nodding at my knitting.

"No. Not at all. I wouldn't wait for someone for that long," I said, stabbing my needle back through the loop. "I mean, it's been what, seventy years? And you're still sitting here?" No one was worth that kind of wait. That kind of trouble. Screw them all.

Etienne rubbed his chin thoughtfully. "Yes, that sounds about right."

I was kind of surprised to hear him admit it. I'd assumed he was one of those out-of-touch sort of ghosts, still thinking that it was 1940. "Then why are you still here? She's gone. She's not coming."

He studied me for a moment. "You've never been in love, have you?"

I didn't respond, just stared at my knitting, cranking out stitches as fast as I could.

"I'm still here because I love her. Because if I had to

wait for a thousand years, I would do it, because she's worth it."

"What if she doesn't feel the same way?" Dammit, there was no reason for me to be tearing up now. What was wrong with me?

"Anna loves me. We will be together one day, and then it will be forever. But even if she didn't, I would still be here, because I made her a promise and she should have someone waiting for her when she comes."

Birds chirped overhead, water trickled in the fountain, and children played on the other side of the park. The sounds of the city were distant in the quiet neighborhood. A few blocks away, an ambulance's siren blared, growing to a crescendo before quickly fading away again.

"You don't know that. You don't know that forever is really forever. And you don't know she loves you. Not really." I wiped away my tears. "People lie all the time. They do horrible things they say are in the name of love, when really it just serves their own purposes. It's just a stupid, made-up word. It doesn't really mean anything."

Etienne put his hand on my shoulder. It was cold, like Micha's, but not as substantial. "Sometimes people do horrible things, thinking it is best. Sometimes they're right, and it's the only option. Sometimes they're wrong. All we can do is forgive them.

"Sometimes, love hits you over the head, or shoots you through the heart. But other times, it lives in the shadows, and hides there until the right moment, and you don't even realize it's there until it's gone, unless you shine the light on it yourself. But once you find it, it's the one thing in this life worth defending. It's the only good reason to go to war—to protect your love so no one else can take it away from you."

By the time he finished, I was crying for real. "This

soldier of yours, give him a chance to defend himself before you put him in front of the firing squad, all right? Liars, cheaters, they're no good and you don't need them, but if all he was trying to do was protect you, then maybe he deserves another chance." He handed me his handkerchief. I wiped my eyes and blew my nose.

When I opened my eyes again, there was someone watching us—a woman, in her mid-twenties, in a floral dress with a flared skirt. At first I thought vintage, but then I realized that no, that dress wasn't secondhand. On her head was a little blue hat with a veil. A very familiar, distinctive hat. I thought back, trying to remember where I'd seen it.

*The old woman reading on the bench.* That *was Anna?*

Etienne stood up, grinning from ear to ear. "Anna. You finally made it."

She held out a hand to him. "I'm sorry, love. I got held up. I hope it wasn't too horrible."

He laced his fingers through hers and pulled her close, kissing each cheek slowly. "No. You're worth it." He offered her his arm, looking back over his shoulder at me.

"Think about it, Evie Cappelli," he said, leading his love off toward the Mountain. When I blinked, they vanished.

I looked down. I was still holding his sodden handkerchief. Then it, too, slowly began to fade, like mist on a pond evaporating in the sun.

Sniffling, I set down my project and walked a slow circuit around the monument. There, near the bottom of the left-hand column. Etienne Passard. One of the few French names listed for a neighborhood that for decads has been predominantly Anglophone.

"You're waiting for someone who doesn't exist anymore," I said quietly. "I'm not her, and I probably never will be. I can just be me, and that's full of flaws. I'm not strong, or brave. Half of the time I wish I didn't even wake up in the morning."

A hand at my waist. Micha pulled me into a light embrace. "I know. But that's the thing about reincarnation—I get to fall in love with you all over again, every time. And each one is different, and each one is the same, and every single time you surprise me with how strong you are, what you're capable of."

"And every time it ends badly."

"But this time, you've got an advantage."

I looked up at him, my head on his shoulder.

"This time, you've got me. I'm not going anywhere. I'm not leaving, I'm not betraying you. I had to keep the secret, because it was important you found out on your own. But from here out, there are no secrets. There's nothing I can't or won't tell you if you ask. Hell, if you'd asked me before, I would have told you, but you didn't know."

"I'm still mad at you."

"I know." He folded me into a hug and kissed my forehead. "I'm okay with that. I wanted to tell you. I'm sorry I couldn't. That I didn't."

The light began to turn golden orange as the sun dropped lower on the horizon. It glinted off the silver in his hair and turned his curls a brilliant copper. I reached up to give one of them a light tug.

"Why are you so real to me, when no one else even knows you're here?" I wondered aloud. Right then, I didn't even care if I looked like a loon, standing there in an empty embrace, tugging on hair that wasn't there.

"I don't know," he replied honestly. He sighed. "I

thought it would be enough for you to see me, to be able to talk to you. But the longer we go on like this, the more I wish I wasn't just a shade."

"Come on, Pinocchio. Let's go home."

# Chapter Eleven
## Evadne

Micha and I walked hand-in-hand back to Izzy's, but we never made it inside. Waiting on the front step was Traverse, a giant tarantula perched on her shoulder and an owl sitting on the rail.

In terse French she said, "I've been waiting for you. Dr. Kelly grows impatient. We have given you more than enough time to consider our offer, and even to reconsider it. It is time to make your choice."

I clenched my hands into fists. In stubborn English I replied, "What is wrong with you people? Why can't you just leave me alone? I never did anything to you!"

Traverse slowly descended the steps to join me on the sidewalk. Micha stood at my back, lending silent support. There wasn't much he could do against a physical threat.

My mind raced as she approached, my thoughts forming total nonsense. Why was I even fighting this? For months, I'd wanted to die. I'd thought about it every day; the only way out for me. But somehow, along the way, I'd discovered I had reasons to live, however small.

"Let Izzy go."

She laughed.

"Let her go, and I'll come with you."

For the first time, I saw Traverse smile. I wished she hadn't.

She held out a hand. When she uncurled her fingers, the scarlet-bodied spider stood there. Before I could move, Traverse threw it down against the pavement, but instead of a bug hitting the concrete, it was Izzy, sprawled on the front steps in her red party dress.

"Izzy!" I tried to run to her, but Traverse caught me, pulling me back.

"We had a deal."

"No, let me go! Izzy!" I couldn't tell if she was breathing. "What did you do? You've hurt her!"

With all of the force in her stout body, Traverse pushed me back, planting one palm on my forehead. "Be quiet! Your time will come soon enough."

I tried to snap back at her, but couldn't. There was something covering my mouth. The more I struggled, the more I found I couldn't move. When I looked down, a thick, white cocoon was rapidly enveloping me from the toes up.

"I should have done this sooner. Much less trouble," my captor said as the silk covered my eyes. With the thick, gummy mess over my nose and mouth, I couldn't breathe. I struggled, gasping. Just before I passed out, Traverse snapped her fingers, and Izzy's unconscious form once again became a spider.

***

I don't know how she managed to get me anywhere without anyone noticing, but while we were in transit the cocoon sent me into a dream—no, a memory. One of Evadne's.

"Yes, that's the charm for a safe childbirth there, and the one next to it will protect children from harm," I explained to the woman admiring my wares.

She ran a finger down the length of intricately braided cord threaded with beads. "I'll take two of these," she said, bouncing the baby on her hip. He scrunched up his face, a sure sign a piercing scream was about to follow.

I held out one of the charms with its shiny trinkets and finger-length fringe to him, and his face relaxed into a smile as he grabbed it from my hand and began to play with it.

His mother sighed with relief.

"See, it's working already," I told her with a smile.

She thanked and paid me, then moved off to the next stall with her other son in tow.

I smiled and greeted the next customer, the conversation flowing easily between us as I prepared a special charm for her to protect her husband, a soldier.

"You're doing well today," said the other novice watching the stall with me. "That's how many charms sold, and it's not even time for lunch yet?"

"Almost thirty. I'm going to run out soon if this keeps up."

I counted the remainder, rearranging them on the table. Normally a temple of Hekate wouldn't be associated with such things, but they'd become something of a specialty. People came from all over when they heard about my charms. I'd taught the other girls to make them, but people still insisted mine were the best. Some even swore the bandages I made healed their wounds faster, or the tunics protected them from harm. I didn't put any stock in those claims, but thanked the goddess she'd chosen to smile on our tiny temple.

Hekate didn't have many dedicated followers. Her

path frightened many, but I knew no other way. I'd been raised in the temple and taught the ways of the priestesses from the time I could walk. When I received my menses, I chose to take my first vows, officially making the life my choice. In just over a year, I would be able to receive my final orders and become a full-fledged priestess.

Until a year ago, the order had been small and poor, our duties consisting primarily of aiding travelers on the dark and dangerous road just outside of the village. We kept a flame lit at all times to guide sailors through the fog that frequently covered our tiny island. We provided food and shelter for those in need. We also handled all of the funeral rites in the village, and for unlucky travelers.

My charms began as offerings, a token for the ferryman and a spell to protect the deceased soul. From there it had grown, and so had our income. A second dormitory was underway to house all the girls wishing to become priestesses, and learn the magic I had somehow mastered.

"Evadne! There he is," hissed Koritto, leaning in close.

I followed her gaze to where he stood, then looked away quickly.

"What are you blushing for? Catch his eye!" she giggled.

"I can't. I'm sworn."

"You're not a priestess yet. They make us novices first so that we still have the option to marry. And he would make an excellent husband," she said, waggling her eyebrows in the direction of the handsome soldier.

"You don't know that," I chided, turning back to my work. "For all you know he could be a drunkard who mistreats his women and gambles away every drachma he earns." But he did have a very nice smile.

"Well, now is your chance to find out. He's headed this way."

Before I could object, Koritto busied herself with another customer and left me to deal with the trio of soldiers who approached.

"I—Hello. What can I do for you?" I said, pasting my cheerful smile back in place.

"We're just looking. We wanted to see what all the fuss was about. Everyone's been talking about the temple of Hekate since we got here," said the shortest one. He had dark hair and eyes and a wiry build. At first glance he looked like an unlikely soldier, easily picked off, but when he moved there was a solidity to his muscles that belied his small frame; he might go down, but it wouldn't be easy and he'd likely take his attacker with him.

The part of me that was still in the present recognized him and his companions with a start. I couldn't remember the last time I'd seen my cousin Isaiah, but it was his soul looking back at me from the small warrior's eyes. The tallest member of the group was none other than Adam.

"Really? That's gratifying to hear. We do our best for the community. Perhaps these might be of interest to you." I pointed out the charms for protection in battle, explaining how they worked. "Just tie it onto your belt, or around your wrist, and the gods will grant their blessing on you."

"Do these really work?" asked the one who would later be reincarnated as Adam. His hair was unruly, skin tanned, as though both had spent too much time in the sun and wind.

"I've never received any complaints."

"You're the one who makes these?" Micha asked, looking impressed.

I nodded, unable to speak. It seemed even in this

former life, he could render me speechless.

Adam leaned against the table. "We were told you can make a shirt that is better than armor. Is that so?"

I chose my words carefully. "I've been told some of the men who wore shirts made from my cloth were very fortunate in battle, but I do not choose who the gods will bless. My charms are one thing; I leave offerings for the gods and work each one with a specific intent. The fabric…I weave it just as any other woman would. I do not know why it would be special."

Koritto, having finished with her customer, saw me floundering, and came to my rescue. "Evadne is one the gods look down on and smile. Sometimes I swear she must have the blessings of both Hekate and Athena, the lucky girl." She giggled coyly. "Now, what is it that brings three fine warriors like yourselves to our little village? We're peaceful here, but it seems like there have been an awful lot of soldiers about lately."

"Orders from the King," Isaiah explained. "It seems Attika may invade any time."

"But we're peaceful with them. Their ships need our island." Located at the very tip of southern Greece, Aegina was the primary stopping point for almost all sea traffic both to and from the mainland.

"Our treaties are still intact, but the people are saying their king has gone mad, that he is searching for Athena's treasure. He believes it will be found on Aegina."

Micha cut off his friend. "It's probably nothing," he said quickly. "We've just been sent as a precaution."

"How long will you be staying?" Koritto asked.

I elbowed her forcefully in the ribs, but she ignored me.

They shrugged. "Until our orders change."

"Well, then you should come to the temple. We

always have a hot meal for weary travelers," she gushed, batting her eyes at the three of them.

"We're not really travelers…."

"But you are far from home, are you not? Please, allow us to make you feel welcome." Her finger skimmed over the back of Adam's hand.

"Koritto!" I shot her a significant look. What was she thinking? We were supposed to be dedicated to Hekate, not Aphrodite!

The soldiers merely laughed. "Perhaps we will, then…if you'll be there?" Micha looked directly at me when he asked.

I felt my face color, deeper than it ever had before. "I—well—"

"Of course she'll be there." Koritto placed her hands on my shoulders. "Won't you, Evadne?"

I nodded, not trusting my voice. I stared at my hands, trying to tame the heat in my cheeks.

The other two had already begun to wander off, but Micha lingered. "Evadne." He rolled my name around on his tongue, as though testing the flavor of a new wine.

"I'll see you there, then."

The scene changed. Spring became winter and the village center turned into a rural landscape. From a hill, the entire town was laid out below, the sea sparkling beyond. The sun was out and the air cool, but not unpleasant with my shawl around my shoulders. I sat with my spinning on a large rock, enjoying the quiet and the solitude.

Arms encircling my waist and a kiss on my neck were the first sign I wasn't, in fact, alone. With one hand remaining at my hip, he came around to sit beside me. The handsome soldier from the market, now *my* soldier. Micha.

"You're a ways out today," he observed.

"Who told you I was here?"

"Koritto, of course."

*Of course.* I rolled my eyes. She was about as discreet as the acrobats who entertained in the city center. If the temple accepted her after her novice period was over, she'd make a terrible priestess of Hekate. But she was a good friend and impossible to be angry with.

"She's worried about you."

I shook my head. "She shouldn't be."

"What's bothering you?"

I offered him a smile and kissed his cheek. "It's nothing."

He smoothed one of the braids back from my face. "You can tell me. I'm your betrothed."

I leaned into his touch. "I don't know. It's just a feeling. I feel something bad is coming, that I should be watching the horizon…but it's nothing. Our peace with Attika remains intact. The temple is doing well, and we are safe."

"But something feels wrong?"

"It's in the air. I can't explain it." I smoothed the wool over my lap. "It's as if panic and destruction are lurking, just waiting to be blown in the next time the wind changes." Sometimes, I thought I saw images of destruction in the magic tapestry in the temple, but only the High Priestess was trained to interpret the signs in the tapestry.

When I tried to explain the feeling to Koritto, who was my closest friend and a sister in every way but blood, she told me I was imagining things—that I was too serious and needed to do something just for fun before I turned into a withered up old hag and Micha wouldn't want to marry me.

For a moment, I thought he would do the same, but he didn't. He looked to the horizon, then back at me, and pulled me a little closer.

"You haven't heard something, have you?" I set my spinning down anxiously.

He shook his head. "No, nothing like that. Just rumors, but who hasn't heard those lately? I've heard everything from Athens being invaded by sorceresses who are controlling the king's mind to civil unrest to everything being a rumor, and all is well."

"What do you think is true?"

Micha considered me, then gently pried my spindle from my fingers. He took my hands and drew me to my feet. "I think we both work too much. I think maybe," he kissed my neck again, "we could use a little bit of a distraction." His hands moved to my hips, and mine found the belt of his chiton. I wrapped the cord around my hand as his lips moved to my mouth. My free arm went around his neck.

Lips and tongues meshed. I dug my fingers into his hair, leaning into him, but when he started to tug at the pin fastening my peplos at the shoulder I pushed him back.

"I'm sorry. I shouldn't have…" he said, releasing me.

I looked away, but didn't move my hand from his chest. "A little longer." I sighed. We planned to marry in the spring, but until then I had my obligations to Hekate, and could not be with a man.

His sigh echoed my own. He took a step back and faced the shoreline, running his hands through his curls and clasping them behind his head. "I just *had* to go and fall for a priestess," he lamented, a smile teasing the edges of his lips. "And one who takes her vows so seriously! Next time, I'll have to find a priestess of

Aphrodite."

"You will not," I said, punching his shoulder lightly. "As if I would let there be a next time. And aren't you the one who said I was worth the wait?"

He dropped his arms to wrap one around me. "For as long as it takes." He kissed my forehead. "Just not too long," he added quickly, as though I might get ideas.

Laughing, I rested my head on his shoulder. "I promise. As soon as I'm released from my vows to Hekate, I will make them to you. You should count yourself lucky. Were I dedicated to Artemis or Athena, I would not be allowed to marry at all, and could only leave the temple in shame."

"Well, we can't have that, now can we?" he asked. Forehead to forehead, we stood in each other's warmth, the tension between us torture.

Pulling back ever so slightly, my words died in my mouth when I saw the horizon and the shadow building there.

"What is that?"

Micha's entire body tensed against mine, the affection draining out. We were so close I could feel the fear flood in to replace it.

"Warships."

***

Myself again, I floated in darkness, a gray mist backed by nothingness. Drifting, formless, I rolled to one side like debris in the St. Laurence and spied the only light. A single torch, planted in the ground I couldn't see. It gave me just enough of a directional bearing to stand upright, or at least float vertically instead of horizontally, more like a ghost and less like a corpse.

The torch attracted more than just me. There was another figure on the other side, her face blocked by the flames. All I could see was the long gray of her robes, blending into the fog, and her pale, graceful arms. Dark hair hung over her shoulders, but I couldn't be sure of the exact color.

The mist was so cold it drew goosebumps from my arms. Faint voices taunted me from somewhere in the distance—a faraway scream, a whisper in my ear. Forget walls and ears; this mist had eyes and they were all on me.

I shivered, hugging myself. Barefoot, in jeans and a tank top, the cold pulled the blood from my limbs, making my skin as pale as bleached linen, the scars on my forearms standing out as two brilliant red streaks.

"Who are you?" I asked through chattering teeth. "Where am I?"

"You are in the mist," my companion replied unhelpfully.

I couldn't believe she wasn't cold. We were both way underdressed for the weather—if you could call it that.

"Okay, that's nice. Now tell me how to get out of here."

"You will leave soon. But I have called you here for a purpose."

My wrists began to ache from the cold. The pain dragged slowly, all the way down to my elbow. Yelping, I held out my arms to see the scars were scars no more, now open and oozing blood. It rushed out faster and faster, spilling over my hands and dribbling onto my jeans. I heard a hiss when it hit the ground, the mist parting just enough for me to see it sizzling where it made contact.

"It hurts, doesn't it?" she said.

"Help me!" I panicked, beginning to feel faint, but then she held out her hands to display the same marks. Blood overflowed from the gashes, creating rivulets. A red Niagara.

She came around the torch so I could see her clearly, and found myself looking at my own face.

# Chapter Twelve
## Grafted Together

She was dressed in the costume of the Ancient Greeks, fastened at the shoulder with bronze pins that looked like coins—round, with faces stamped on them. Who it was supposed to be, however, I had no idea, and I was too preoccupied with bleeding to death to really care. Around her waist, a belt of braided leather tipped with copper cinched in the loose, flowing garment. No, not a belt. A whip.

Evadne.

The blood was everywhere. I had nothing to wrap around the cuts. My arms hurt like fire—

"Not like fire," she smiled wryly. "I've felt that. It's much worse."

I was too shocked to respond. My fingers were practically numb. I pressed my arms into the fabric of my thin tank top in a fruitless attempt to stop the bleeding.

"Good. You're fighting. That's an improvement."

"What are you smiling for? Are you crazy?"

But she just stood there, as wounded as myself, with that stupid, stupid cat-that-ate-the-cream smile.

"I know how to make it stop," she said.

"Great for you. Got any bandages?" I swayed on my

feet, but my clone didn't seem to notice or care. Instead of being helpful, she started spouting cryptic riddles.

"Damaged souls make poor heroes. Rejoin the halves to make a whole. No one can take away what is a part of you."

"That's nice." Was it getting darker or was it just me? I listed to the left.

She caught my elbows to keep me on my feet. Nose to nose, she said again, "Rejoin the halves to make a whole."

I met her eyes as my vision flickered like the torch. Our blood mingled on my arms. It drenched my skin. Giddy, I wished I had my sewing kit.

*Rejoin the halves to make a whole.*

Our blood, mixing. The girl with my face, Evadne. Which blood was a part of me, now? It all seemed to be going away rather quickly. Our arms pressed together in a morbid promise. Blood sisters. Soul sisters.

My thoughts lost cohesion around the same time everything went black.

***

*Both.*

That was the answer, I realized, sucking in air like I'd been underwater for too long. I coughed and hacked, patting myself down while spots danced in front of my eyes. It took a few passes to convince myself the blood was gone.

Because that was the answer—both streams of blood belonged to me. *Evadne.* The lost incarnation, the one I'd forgotten somehow. The one who knew and loved Micha. The one who planned to be with him before it all fell apart.

My hands and wrists still ached, like I'd been knitting for too long without a break. When I gave my arm warmers a tug, I saw my scars were faded, less noticeable than they had been even that morning.

"Evie!" Micha knelt beside me.

"Good, she's awake. At least you didn't suffocate her like the last one," said a voice above my head.

I looked up and saw a new face. Younger, plain but pleasant, with brown hair pulled back in a bun and glasses with thick black frames. Dressed casually in jeans and a soft blue T-shirt, she made a nice change from the Athenian women I'd been seeing, who were always polished and professional.

Well, except for Anaïs Traverse and her sour, stoic face and dowdy, dated outfits.

She glared at me through her cat-eye spectacles. "The last one was trouble," she replied, her eyes narrowing. "And if she hadn't been such a weakling to begin with, she would have been fine." She said it as if it was my fault "the last one" had suffocated inside the cocoon.

The younger woman didn't respond, except for a distasteful expression Traverse couldn't see as her underling bent over me. She used a thick copper knife to cut me free. Micha gripped my hands, clearly invisible to them now that he wasn't in Hekate's territory. I held on to him, but didn't dare speak out loud. I wanted to tell him what I'd seen. Evadne's memories mingled with my own, slightly out of sync but there. Greece. War. Magic. Micha. It was all there—a disorganized mess I would have to sift through later. For now, my heart was pounding and I was still a little short of breath, but I had more important things to worry about than the fact that my former fiancé was now a ghost who didn't even remember being alive.

The only way to describe the room we were in was a dungeon. Stone floor and walls, roughly cut, with iron fastenings on the wooden braces holding up the ceiling. A bank of flickering fluorescent lights overhead weren't enough to chase away the gloom.

Assuming we were still on the island, that meant we could only be in Old Montreal, near the Old Port. The oldest part of the city, it was now a high-class tourist attraction, with lots of street food, performances, and souvenir shops.

Of course, none of it was visible from my current vantage point. Just four plain walls, a heavy door, and two stern faces.

And a whole lot of spider silk.

It still clung to my clothes and hair, but at least it was off my face. I tried to brush it away, but it was too sticky.

The second woman grabbed me around my upper arm and lifted me to my feet awkwardly, my legs tangled in the remnants of the cocoon. She sliced away at them, freeing me roughly, and then pulled me to the door. It was a relief to see it was open.

"Where are you taking me?" I asked. The pressure on my arm eased, now that the woman knew I would follow her—anything to get out of the dungeon—but my eyes darted around the corridor, looking for a means of escape. I had two choices, as far as I could see: back into the dungeon, or follow my captors up the stairs at the end of the hall to the ground floor and hope for escape there.

"Upstairs. Need to get you cleaned up. Then you'll be meeting with Dr. Kelly, and we'll get you set up for the ceremony."

"What about my aunt?"

"What about her?"

"Where is she?"

My guide shrugged in a *don't know, don't care* fashion. "Dr. Kelly will answer your questions. It's just my job to get you ready." She pursed her lips and I realized with a start it was the girl who had tried to stand up for me on the rooftop. I barely recognized her without the fancy hairdo and contacts.

I glanced over my shoulder at Traverse, who followed behind, as expressionless as ever. Her cold, golden-brown eyes made me shudder. Licking my dry lips I turned back to the front, praying for a moment alone with my escort. Maybe I could still talk her out of this craziness.

Micha stuck close at my back as we followed the woman up to the first floor, and then the second. I caught glimpses of outside through the windows, but nothing clear—a stone wall, an empty street. I couldn't see any signs, couldn't pause long enough for a better look. It was dark out, the limited light of the Old Port working against me.

*Pay attention.* The decor fit roughly with the period in which it was built. Worn rugs on the floor, minimal electricity. Lights hidden inside of old sconces, nothing overhead. Except for those lights, everything else appeared to be original. The doors and windows were all old-fashioned, made of heavy wood and bubbled glass.

On the landing, we passed a tapestry of a hunt scene. Faded from the vibrant original to watery pinks and pale blues, the hunters surrounded their quarry, an elegant white stag. I empathized with the poor thing.

There was a tear in the fabric just below the rear hooves. Reflexively, I reached out to run my fingers over it as we passed. The threads knit themselves back together, raw edges rejoining, broken ends spinning themselves back together.

The entire sequence took about three seconds, but it

was enough. I don't think the woman gripping my arm noticed. I couldn't say the same for Traverse.

Down another hallway and through a door to a bedroom. Utilitarian, it was obviously a guest room of some kind, though I couldn't think of anyone who would have both dungeons and a guest room. The Dragon Lady held the door open for us, then bolted my guard and I inside.

There was a white robe laid out on the bed, just like the ones the initiates had been wearing for the ceremony, and Evadne had worn in my vision. It was extra-long, brilliant white. Linen. Two gold pins already secured the shoulders. This time, I could see the faces pressed into the metal: Athena. Her profile, identifiable by the helmet.

"Okay. Take those off. We've got a bath waiting for you," the woman said, gesturing to the attached bathroom. Clearly a later add-on, it was updated with marble everything and a fancy claw-foot tub. The fluffiest towels I'd ever seen waited on the brass bar just above it.

"I know you don't agree with this. Please, help me—"

"Shut up," she snapped, eyes flashing. Then she sighed. "They aren't going to kill you, if that's what you think. Dr. Kelly is just trying to scare you."

"She seemed pretty damn serious to me!"

"Look, she's kind of mad at you and your aunt, I guess because you turned her down. She likes to think she's all-powerful and all that. But really, we just need your help." She handed me the peplos. "Play along and you'll get out fine, okay?"

"You're sure?"

She frowned, doubt flitting across her eyes. "Yeah. Completely."

I was filthy and sweaty and still covered in spider

gunk. I turned toward the lure of hot water and soap.

Her voice came behind me: "You have ten minutes. After that, I'm coming in. And don't shut the door." She braced it open, leaving a six-inch gap. Just enough to see if I was in the tub. I didn't like it, but I didn't fight her. I stepped back from the door long enough to remove my clothes, then slipped into the water. For once, I didn't mind the fact that Micha didn't leave the room.

Closing my eyes, I slipped beneath the surface. I didn't have long. Ten minutes to sift through the mess in my head and find something useful, like a plan.

Unless you've received a brain dump from one of your past lives yourself, I can't really describe the feeling. Faces mingled, some clearer than others. Information on food and festivals mixed with long dead politics and images of ships and buildings and countrysides. The taste of figs—which I'd never even had outside of Fig Newtons—blended into a strong wine, which recalled a summer festival and a stolen moment with Micha behind a potter's stall that made me blush. It had been the first time he said he loved me, in any lifetime.

Breaking the surface, I sucked down another lungful of air. I wiped warm water from my eyes, pushed my hair out of the way, and reached for the soap. I scrubbed the grime off like it would help remove the layers I didn't need and bring out the ones I did.

Micha knelt beside the tub. He took my hand, eyes anxiously searching my face. Had he seen what I'd seen? Charms sold in the marketplace that had people lining up. Bandages that healed the wounded. Clothing that protected the wearer.

Evadne had more secrets than just that, though she didn't truly understand it—not that I had any better ideas. Magic was still so new to me, I kept having to tell myself not to think about it too hard—or else I would start to doubt. It was too late to be questioning now.

It started with her spinning; the first household chore a child learned in Ancient Greece. Drawing out the wool and spinning it tight, winding it onto the shaft of the spindle.

The youngest girls at the temple cleaned and picked debris from the wool before it could be dyed and spun. From a young age, hers had come out the cleanest. The threads she spun the smoothest and most even—the fibers becoming almost sentient in her hands, following her every desire.

It was like when I repaired the tapestry. The fibers, the individual strands within the threads, wanted to be whole. When I touched the gash, I could feel how much they wanted to join together again, just as my blood and Evadne's had mingled. Two halves of the same thing. On their own, they were useless, but together they formed something much stronger. Better.

When she wove those threads into fabric, or sewed them into clothing or embroidered their edges, she brought out the magic in them. I needed a little bit of that.

Lathering my hair with rose-scented shampoo, I massaged out the spider silk. It twisted itself around my wrist. When I pulled my hand free, I had a perfect loop of silk, untangled, waiting patiently for my next move.

Micha squeezed my hand. We had a plan.

***

My guard's name was Vera. After barging in to pull me out of the tub, she dried me off like a particularly bothersome piece of silverware, then drove me back into the bedroom, where I was wrapped in the peplos.

"Get her talking. Distract her," Micha said over her shoulder as she tied me into the drapey fabric.

"So, um, what can you tell me about this ceremony? Seems like a pretty big to-do," I said as she forced me onto the stool in front of the mirror. Grabbing a brush, she ran it roughly through my hair, ripping out more knots than she untangled. I flinched, but tried not to complain.

"It is. Dr. Kelly will call on Athena. Once she reclaims her blessing from you, then you will become the vessel, capable of channeling her messages once again."

"Sorry, they want me to do what?"

"There's a legend that in ancient times the cult of Athena had a magical tapestry, which could tell the future. It was a created by one of the Blessed of Athena, a weaver. But the tapestry has been lost. Dr. Kelly wants to create a new one, so we can obtain our rightful place."

"Rightful place?"

Vera looked at me like I was stupid. "In society. In the world. Do you know that in Western society, women make up less than half of all legislators? We make less than men, and control less than one percent of the world's overall wealth?

"If we had a way of seeing and shaping the future, do you know what we could do with it? We could stop wars before they started. Create economic empires. Prevent epidemics. We could *finally* lead."

"So this whole thing is basically a big feminist rally? I mean, I'm all for equality, but—"

"This isn't about equality! It's about taking back what should rightfully be ours! Look at the mess men have made of the world!"

I choked on a bitter taste in my mouth. I wasn't opposed in the slightest to their goals—equal rights, equal pay. Stopping war. But they way they were going about it was wrong. Killing people? Kidnapping? Turning people into bugs?

I could feel her really ramping up for a good long rant, so I tried to change the subject. "So I'm supposed to make a new one, then?"

Vera nodded, giving one of the braids a stronger tug than was necessary. "Yes. But first you must dedicate your life to the service of Athena, or else she won't share her secrets with you."

"Then what was all of that talk about sacrificing me?"

Vera hesitated. "Once you become the vessel, your life as Genevra Cappelli will be over. You'll be part of the society, Athena's voice on earth."

"I am the Metatron," I said in my best Alan Rickman impersonation.

"What?"

"Don't tell me that name doesn't ring a bell for you?" I sighed dramatically. "You people."

"What the hell are you talking about?"

I sighed again, this time in resignation. Clearly the Athenians weren't fans of pop culture. Not that I could talk. I got most of my references from Izzy, which meant they were mostly out of date, anyway.

"So what you're telling me is you want to summon the goddess of war in order to start world peace?"

"This isn't war. And she's a goddess of tactics and strategy. It wouldn't make sense for Dr. Kelly to kill you for some stupid grudge when keeping you alive serves the greater good."

I turned to face her. "Do you really believe that?"

Vera's face was grim and serious. "Yes."

*Too bad I don't.*

Vera finished my hair and makeup. When she was

done, she knocked twice on the door. Outside, two more women waited. One of them was in a more ornate version of my outfit, with more embroidery. She held a spear. The other was a uniformed police officer.

Switching to French, Vera said, "She's ready. Take her to the ballroom."

The guards didn't manhandle me the way Vera had, but the one with the spear watched me like a particularly hungry hawk as we followed the cop down to the first floor. There was a large, open room not far from basement door.

The ballroom was about the size of a hockey rink, with high ceilings and an ornate wood floor. At the center of the room was what looked like a giant bronze goblet filled with fire. Around the outside of the basin were images of Athena doing great works—teaching mortals to weave, conquering her enemies, sitting beside Zeus on Mt. Olympus. Paintings and tapestries of similar motifs hung on the walls. Some of them were directly from Greek mythology; others were more like historical girl-power images, women triumphing over their oppressors. I spied at least two different versions of Judith and Holofernes, with Artemisia Gentileschi playing a significant role in the decor.

On the far side of the room was a dais, backed by a floor-to-ceiling marble sculpture of Athena in full battle regalia, and flanked by two more women in Greek costume with spears. I wondered if they realized how utterly ridiculous they looked, until the one behind me prodded me in the back with the business end of her spear to urge me forward. After that, they didn't seem quite so ridiculous.

Other Sisters milled in and out. The cop turned me over to the two waiting by the dais, so I was surrounded by three women in outdated clothing.

Clenching my fists at my side, I waited anxiously while the room was prepared. Someone closed the curtains, plunging the room into darkness except for the Goblet of Fire. The thought made me giggle from nerves.

"If you're trying to get me to sign up for the Tri-wizard Tournament, I think I'll pass. I'd rather not die and come back as a sparkly vampire."

"Silence!" snapped the guard who had followed me from upstairs. Shorter than the others, she only came up to my nose, but somehow managed to be the most intimidating of the trio. Her hair was darker and she looked like she spent the most time in the sun. Her features were too strong to be called pretty, but I suppose she might have been attractive if she hadn't been looking at me like she wanted to make an Evie-kebob and roast me over the open flame.

The other two looked like models: fair skin with a golden glow, one with honey brown hair done up in braids more elaborate than mine; and the other a blond, curls twisted around a gold cord balanced precariously on the back of her head. The brunet stared straight ahead, but the blond offered me a cold glare before going back to staring into the middle distance.

Two more women in Greek garb came in to light the candles scattered around the room. The smoke drifted upward to a vent in the ceiling—the only sign of modernity in the room. Someone spread a cloth over the altar and laid out a cup and two candles, lighting them both. Someone else brought an elaborately carved bookstand and settled a scroll onto it, rolling it open to a specific point, and holding it in place with two thin weights. They set out a shallow bowl near the fire to complete the setup.

"What do you think?" Dr. Kelly appeared in the door. She was also in Greek clothing, but her peplos was embroidered, trimmed in gold, and her short hair covered by a thin, flowing shawl. From the belt at her waist hung a thick sheath, the handle of a dagger sticking out. Her wrists were adorned with bracelets, but when she held out her hands, I could see the owl tattoo with perfect clarity.

"We wanted to perform the ceremony at the party, of course, so everyone could take part, but this will work out even better. No prying eyes. We can do things properly this way."

Her eyes practically glowed, and I wasn't sure if it was from the lighting or if it was just plain psychotic bloodlust. I nearly said as much, but I bit my tongue. As the room was beginning to fill, now was not the time to start pissing people off. Especially not when there were three people within arm's reach who would happily skewer and roast me like a marshmallow.

I took a step toward her. The tiny guard held out her spear to stop me, but I held up a hand. "I'll go quietly. I'll do what you want. I won't fight. But you have to turn Izzy back and let her go, first. Whatever I might have done in another life, whatever she did, she's got nothing to do with this now. Keeping her here doesn't help you."

Kelly snorted dismissively. "Let her go? After all of this? I don't think so. She'd go straight to the police."

"And tell them what, exactly? What could she say that they would actually believe? No one knows she's missing. I've got a history of mental illness; if she told the cops and they looked into her background, they'd probably say I got it from her, that it was the delusion of a damaged mind. And I'm sure you have measures in place—alibis, whatever—that would keep you from being arrested for kidnapping. Or maybe you just resort to using dirty cops for that," I said, glancing at the cop-guard as she re-entered the room, this time sans uniform, dressed like all the others in Athenian haute couture. If I paid more attention to the news, I'd probably recognize politicians and other important people from around the province, but for the moment I could only concentrate on Kelly, Traverse, and Vera. The others blended together.

Kelly's face clouded, her eyes narrowing, and I felt like they'd stabbed me with one of those spears, pinned me to the floor like some kind of insect on display. An experiment for her and her students to play around with and dissect at will. "We don't need to resort to things like bribery. Not when we are in the right. Besides, once we succeed, it won't matter. We will be the ones in power. We'll simply capture her again, so what's the point?"

"That's the deal. Let her go, or else I'll fight. And you don't want me to fight." I tried to make it sound as threatening as I could, like I actually stood a chance of walking out, surrounded as I was by women with spears. Even without the spears, twenty-to-one wasn't great odds. In fact, they kind of sucked. I suddenly wished I had more self-defense training than battling faux-fur giants at Tam-Tams, instead of being a hopeless couch potato. "I'm the one you need, not her. And since you'll be the all-powerful ones, in charge of everything, it'll take you what, five minutes to bring her back in? What's it matter to you? But it would make me feel better to know that before I go, she's got a chance. Consider it a head start. It wouldn't be sporting otherwise, right?"

Kelly looked me up and down, as though trying to decide if I was actually stupid enough to try to outsmart her. I wasn't; I knew when it came to tactics, I was hopelessly outclassed. But maybe, just maybe, if I couldn't do anything, then Adam and Izzy could.

*Adam*. He had no idea what was going on. I wondered briefly how long it would be before they came for him.

I spared a glance for Micha; he nodded. I didn't know much about ghosts, or spirits, or anything like that. If they killed me, using my soul to feed their goddess, then my only hope was Micha would choose to stay behind since I wouldn't be reborn. Maybe he could somehow pass on a message to Adam, and to my family, about what happened and what the Athenians were planning.

"You are forgetting one thing," Kelly said at last. "You do have another option. One last chance to join us. Dedicate yourself fully to Athena, devote your magic and your talents to her. Reject the outside world and its temptations, and work for us, rather than against us. With your abilities, you would be a princess, revered above all others as the blessed of Athena."

"And what happens when I've fulfilled my duties? When I've completed the tapestry?" Judging by the glare Kelly gave me, Vera was about to be in even more trouble.

"Your life belongs to us. Your rewards will come through us. You will have work. A purpose. A place in the power structure of the new world we create. The Blessed are rare. It would be a shame to waste one, but blood, sweat, or tears—we'll wring the magic from you one way or another. It's your choice how we proceed."

"Spend my life with you? No thanks. That's a fate worse than death." My fists clenched at my sides, digging into the thick material of my peplos.

"Suit yourself," she snapped, her face twisting with anger. "Bind her," she said to the petite guard before turning to address the assembly. "Places, everyone. Tonight, we summon a goddess."

# Chapter Thirteen
## Kate and Anpu

I didn't budge. "What about Izzy?"

"Once the goddess is summoned and we have achieved our rightful place, the Legion will be of little use. Why should I allow her a head start when she will die anyway? She's so much quicker to kill as an insect."

"She's not an insect. They're arachnids."

I wasn't sure my plan would work until I put my hand out and *pulled*.

Threads from all over the room tremored. Strays leaped into my hand, twining themselves together. The hem of my robe began to unravel until it was knee length.

Several of the women closest to me stumbled and fell when their dresses did the same. Others lost their balance as they struggled against skirts that suddenly wrapped around their legs or collars that were too tight.

The entire thing wound up in a single dark-colored thread that snapped into my hand like a retractable leash. The long black thread, connected to my old clothes upstairs, *wanted* to be with me. The fibers, worn smooth and soft over the past few years, were loyal like a dog and wanted to help. I allowed myself a brief smile. While I'd been in the bath, I'd used the magic to loosen the fibers, and subtly connected the thread to the hem of my robe.

Of the twenty or so women in the room, however, I was hardly the only one who could control thread. I don't know why it didn't occur to me sooner, since I was in *Athena's* house.

Three of the women, caught caught off guard, simply smoothed down their clothes and reached for their knives, hacking away at the threads. Where they cut, I felt a sharp *twang* as the magic snapped back at me, the fibers no longer under my control.

I knew I didn't have long before they pulled out their own magic. I cut off the flow of energy and moved on to the second part of the plan Micha and I concocted.

When I lashed out, it wasn't with the speed or finesse of Evadne. My hastily constructed whip didn't have the bite or quite the same snap as hers, but I'd used materials that were familiar to me. The cotton and nylon and spandex from my clothes knew what I wanted, and like tiny sheepdogs they corralled the unrulier fibers I'd taken from the others and told them what I needed. I tried to relax and let Evadne's memories take over. I didn't have her muscle memory, but I had her know-how.

It's amazing what you can whip up when you're under pressure.

The first strike hit Kelly on the arm. The second knocked the spear out of the blonde guard's hand as she thrust it in my direction.

My palms grew sweaty and I could already feel the strain in my shoulders. This was so far away from anything I'd ever done—

The whip twisted around one of the other guard's spears. I spun under it, ripping it from her hands. Now I had two weapons.

Another snap to the side, and the whip wrapped itself around my waist, staying in place without a knot, without any effort from me.

I giggled madly, realizing more of the fibers wanted to help me. The spider silk, slick and smooth, but sticky as salt-water taffy, waited patiently, wrapped up with the cotton and giving it extra strength. The sturdy cotton, the blue of worn-in jeans that had molded to the shape of my legs after years of wear, and faded black from a tank top that seldom saw the inside of a dresser. Fibers I had touched nearly every day for months, maybe longer. They felt warm and solid under my hand, waiting to form whatever I desired. The linen, which softened the more it moved and rubbed against the others, was snappy and crisp, making a solid core. The synthetics, man-made, were up for anything with the right encouragement.

With both hands now free to use the spear, I tried to recall the training I'd gotten on the Mountain, such that it was.

"Jab!" Micha ordered. "Left! Block! Look behind you!"

Hearing his voice was just enough to keep my heart from pounding out of my chest. Adrenaline had it going about six times faster than usual.

I planted a kick into one of my attackers' stomachs—Vera, I realized, and felt a little pang of regret. She was new, and enthusiastic, and mostly just following orders. But she was also a True Believer, and for that reason scarier than an open flame in a Victorian cotton mill.

I danced away from a spear thrust, panting slightly. If I made it through this, I would have to work on my cardio. That was looking unlikely, however, as the Sisters closed ranks around me.

Then Traverse appeared, and I knew it was over.

The Legion of spiders began to form out of the darkness. Threads of silk appeared around her hands, floating on tiny drafts of air. The others backed off, hemming us in. Chest heaving, mouth dry, I knew I wouldn't be getting out of that circle.

The shadow began to form at her hand, growing larger and darker until it reached the ground. Thousands of spiders carpeted the floor. I forced myself to look at them, to search for Izzy. I saw all different kinds. Big, horrible wolf spiders and tiny, almost microscopic specimens. A tarantula crawled over someone's shoulder and I shuddered. Big, small, hairy, smooth. Shades of brown and black, and a few exotic multicolored ones, too. More than a few had the hourglass markings of black widows.

I swallowed nervously, the spear quivering in my hand. Beside me, Micha was pale, despite having no blood to begin with.

"Any suggestions?" I mumbled.

His mouth worked. "Get her talking. Stall. I'll see what I can do." He vanished.

*Great. Leave me alone with a room full of psychopaths and venomous spiders. Fabulous.* I wasn't sure which of those options bothered me more.

The spiders advanced on me slowly. I resisted the urge to scream and stomp on them all indiscriminately. For starters, Izzy might be part of the crowd, and I'd hate to kill her by accident. And then there was what Kelly had said—each one was a failure. A girl they'd thought was me over the centuries, but hadn't made the cut. The ones who tried to escape and saw too much. A person.

I backed away from them until I hit the wall. I half expected the Athenians to start chanting *fight, fight!* like some kind of street brawl, but instead they watched silently, the older ones solemn, some with a satisfied smirk on their faces. The younger members, like Vera, stood near the back, bouncing on the balls of their feet for a better view, naked excitement in their eyes.

My eyes locked with Vera's for a brief moment. "Are you all insane? How can you think this is okay? To hunt people down—turn them into bugs and use them to attack people that didn't do anything to you? Are you all so completely brainwashed you'll listen to whatever crazy shit she says?" I gestured with the spear in Kelly's general direction.

If I'd been expecting a flutter of doubt from the crowd, or maybe one or all of them would turn on their leader and help me, then I was disappointed. But I didn't have time to contemplate their lack of moral compass. Distracted by the need to find Izzy, I didn't pay attention to Traverse and her silk. It formed a web all around the room, difficult to see in the dim light and just catching reflections here or there. She'd trapped us. Like a steel fight cage, it locked us in one corner of the room.

More spiders dangled from the web. I looked up to see tiny specks darting back and forth, a few lowering themselves like cat burglars toward me. One of them had a red abdomen, but before I could do anything about it, more silk crept out and wrapped itself around my arms.

Sticky and stiff, I pulled at it but it wouldn't budge. Traverse smiled—the most frightening expression I'd ever seen on her face.

"You're caught, now," she said. "Madge might go easy on you, but I won't. I've had enough of this useless flailing. You aren't even worth sacrificing to the goddess—she'd throw you back!" She cackled, her threads slinking their way farther up my bare arms.

I closed my eyes and concentrated. If I could control

the silk and the cotton in the bathroom, then this should be no problem. Threads were already loose in the air, I just had to take hold of them.

But she was too strong. Those threads, they belonged to her; they bent to her will and no other. They slipped through my awareness like garden snakes through grass, absorbing her malice like a high-quality dye. The only way I'd be able to break it would be if I could tear them away from her.

A horrible memory came to life: the silk wound its way closer and closer. More threads flew from her fingertips, binding my legs and torso as the Legion swarmed around me, crawling up the mummy-like wrappings and adding their own spinning skills to the mix. In moments, I'd been cocooned for the second time in as many hours.

The gossamer reached my shoulders, then my neck. I could feel it in my hair, forming a crown that came down a little lower for every second that ticked by.

Still struggling, I snapped my mouth shut when it reached my lips, and inhaled sharply for what I suspected would be the last time as it began to cover my nose.

I'm not sure if it covered my eyes first, or if I simply blacked out.

* * *

I was starting to think I couldn't just go to sleep or get knocked unconscious anymore without someone deciding to visit me while I was out. I found myself back in the grey mist where I'd met Evadne, surrounded by nothing but fog. It was so thick I could barely see my hand in front of my face, but somewhere up ahead there was light. I stumbled toward it.

The light came from a path lined with torches like the one I'd seen on my last visit. I followed them, something big looming at the end. I couldn't make out what it was until I was practically on the front step.

It was a temple. Evadne's temple. Or at least, the ruined, burnt-out shell of it. Smoke stained the partially collapsed interior. The tapestries were charred ruins, just a few scraps of burnt fabric hanging from the ceiling.

More torches burned in sconces around the room, creating a path toward the back of the building. Feeling I should follow, I did. My footsteps echoed on stone, adding to the eerie feeling that a distant set of eyes were watching.

The air around me was as cold as Micha's skin. I rubbed my arms for warmth.

The torches stopped at the door to the catacombs. I stood stared down into absolute darkness.

*Yes, let's go down and see the dead bodies, shall we?* Yeah, that sounded like a great idea.

"Waking up would be good right now," I said. Nothing. I tried pinching myself, with the same result.

"Right. So down it is." Removing one of the torches from its resting place, I crept toward the stairs, swallowing the fear building in my chest.

The catacombs were solid black my torch barely penetrated. I didn't know where I was supposed to go— only that someone evidently wanted me to keep moving. When I stopped at the bottom of the stairs and tried to go back, I walked into a solid wall. The door was gone.

No place to go but forward, then.

All of this echoed my visions of Evadne, so I tried to remember what she had been looking for.

Everything had been in multiples of nine, I remembered. Nine passages, nine niches. I started counting out loud to chase away the heavy silence, and coughed on the smell of mold and dust.

Ninth shelf down. Ninth skull.

It stared out at me from empty orbits, a wicked grin on its face. I reached for it, hesitated, and then pulled back. The darkness grew even more oppressive. The circle of light trapped me; beyond it was nothing. Not simple darkness—the world ceased to exist outside the glow of my torch. Wherever it was the dream wanted me to go, I had no choice but to follow.

I grabbed the skull and wrenched it quickly to the side. Stone ground on stone as I wiped dirty fingers on my peplos—I was still in the stupid costume Vera had put me in. At least my whip was still around my waist. I might not be great at using it, but it felt kind of nice to know I could defend myself if I needed to.

The wall swung open. Instead of finding the hidden chamber with the gold and the tapestry, however, I found more stairs and a tunnel even darker and more still than the one I was already in.

"Okay, this isn't funny anymore," I told the darkness at large. "I'd like to go home now."

Quiet laughter bubbled up from the staircase. Not mocking, but mirthful, as though someone down there found my fear to be amusing. If I hadn't liked the staircase before, I liked it even less now.

"Is someone there?" I called. I had to try twice, because I couldn't get myself to speak above a whisper the first time.

No answer, but it felt like the darkness was giving me a Cheshire grin, if only I could turn the light in the right place to see it.

I put my foot on the first step, bracing my free hand against the wall for balance. This tunnel was narrower than the last, only a little broader than my shoulders. I felt claustrophobic just looking at it.

"Darling, if you're going to walk the path that will lead you to what you want, you'll have to get used to your own company in close quarters."

The voice was right in my ear, warm breath on my neck. I jerked to the side, swatting at the disembodied voice with the torch. My foot slipped and I went ass over teakettle down the stairs. The torch went flying, bouncing off the stone before extinguishing at the bottom.

Dizzy, bruised, and uncertain if I was still all in one piece, I lay sprawled on the floor and stared at the ceiling, which seemed to roll  from side to side like I was on a boat.

"Sorry, I should have warned you about that first step," said the voice, laughing once again.

I raised my head just enough to get a view of the room I'd tumbled into. High ceilinged, it was clearly a natural cave converted into some kind of throne room. At the far end was a simple throne, black velvet on obsidian, with silver accents resembling stars in the night sky. It was perched on a low dais, but no one was sitting there.

The room was somewhat spartan, but it looked like someone was making an attempt to warm it up. In the corner stacks of artwork leaned against the wall, too far away for me to see the subjects. There were no windows, but there was a tapestry on the wall to my right. If I wasn't mistaken, it was Evadne's tapestry—the one she'd fought so hard to protect. As I looked at it, the images seemed to shift. I rubbed my eyes and let my head fall back to the floor with a *thunk*.

"Ow."

"You're sure about this one?" a new voice asked skeptically. Deeper, male. Accented, though I had no idea where the accent was from. Middle Eastern, maybe.

The woman chuckled. "Oh, don't worry about her. She's still pulling herself together. She'll be fine." She laughed as if at some private joke.

Deciding the floor really wasn't that comfortable once I'd lain on it for a while, I rolled onto my side and managed to sit up stiffly. At least the room wasn't spinning anymore, though I probably still had some bruises.

The speakers were the only other people in the room. A woman with long dark hair cascading loose around her shoulders and the long dress of the Ancient Greeks, and a man. Tall, tan, and muscular, with a shaved head, wearing nothing but a white linen kilt, sandals, and a heavy necklace of black and red stones set in gold.

The pair were playing chess at a card table in the center of the room, and paying me almost no attention. I got to my feet with the aid of the doorframe I'd just fallen through.

"You see, I told you she'd make it." The woman grinned.

The man sighed, reached into his pocket, and produced a gold coin, which he passed over to her.

The woman bounced giddily in her seat, tucking the coin away. With barely a glance at the board, she moved one of her pieces several spaces. "Checkmate!"

With another disgruntled sigh, the man propped his chin in his hand. "You're cheating."

"Am not!" she said. I couldn't tell if she was offended, or if the look of horror on her face was just for show. "It's not my fault you're no good at strategy." She reached over and patted his arm. "Next time we'll get a jigsaw puzzle, how about that?"

"I like puzzles."

She gave him a winning smile. "I know you do, dear." She waved her hand and the game vanished, replaced by a 4,000-piece 3D replica of Big Ben.

With a grin, the man popped the box open and began sorting through the pieces.

The woman rose gracefully from her seat and approached me. "Evadne. Evie. So good to see you again at last." She clasped my hands in both of hers. Over her shoulder, I saw one of the three headed statues from the temple. The central face looked directly at me and winked.

It suddenly clicked who the mysterious woman was. "Oh my god. You're Hekate."

The fabulous smile came back, a contrast from the serious statues I'd seen. She didn't have three heads or the terrifying features some of them did. Actually, she reminded me a bit of Izzy. The coloring was similar, with dark hair and light eyes, but there was something else. Their faces were drastically different. Izzy looked like me, with pointed features that came directly from our Mediterranean ancestry. This woman was soft and symmetrical, young and pretty in a model-like way, but with hidden depths of amusement and cunning lurking beneath her blue eyes.

"I'm so glad you remember me," she gushed, acting like we were old girlfriends. She put one arm around my shoulders, guiding me to the puzzle table. "Ani didn't think you'd make it back here. You had such a rough time of it, but I told him you were my most dedicated servant, and there was no way you would let me down."

"Don't call me Ani," the man sing-songed, carefully snapping a piece onto one of the walls he was constructing. He already had the foundation and one corner completely put together, and was working his way out from there. Off to one side, the top of the clock tower waited patiently for the rest of the building to be finished.

"Of course not, dear." Hekate gave him a peck on the cheek, and led me over to her throne. "Don't mind Anubis, dear. He's been so grouchy ever since they gave his kingdom to Osiris. The movies nowadays don't help matters much. You should have seen what he did when *The Mummy* came out. Locusts, all over LA."

"I don't remember hearing about that…."

She waved a hand dismissively and draped herself over the throne, crossing her legs. It suited her perfectly, as though two halves of a whole were now one again.

"All joking aside, however, I am glad you came," she said.

"Look, no offense or anything, but I wasn't really trying to come here. And if it's all the same to you, I think I've had enough goddesses for one lifetime." Free from her protective arm, I started to back up a little.

"Oh, don't worry. I don't want to hurt you. I like you better alive."

"That's kind of funny, coming from the goddess of death. See, the goddess of war wanted me dead. Or at least enslaved. I really can't imagine you want anything less."

Her face clouded slightly, and I bit my tongue. *Do not piss off the goddess, do not piss off the goddess…* If she really didn't want to kill me, I'd prefer to keep it that way.

She pinned me in place with her eyes. I gulped and froze.

"No offense. Or anything," I squeaked belatedly.

The smile popped back into place as though nothing had transpired. "No worries. But I hope what I propose will help with all of that.

"You have regained your memories, have you not?

Memories of your time in my service."

I nodded. She waited for me to elaborate. "I was in the temple, training. And I made charms."

Her eyes glimmered. "And your young man?"

I blushed. "Micha."

Hekate smiled. "Yes. That's the one."

There were still a few things that didn't make sense. Things, I suppose, I simply didn't remember yet. From the tilt of her head, Hekate was waiting expectantly for me to ask. So I did.

"How… I don't understand the connection…"

"Between the Blessed of Athena, and how you came to be in my service?" She shrugged. "Simple, really. Arachne's husband—Evadne's father—offered his daughter's life to appease Athena, but her nurse took the child out of fear and ran. She died on the journey, and baby Evadne, with no clues to her former life, was left to my temple. She was taken in first as a ward, then as a postulate before beginning her service.

"She was very good, you know. Very dedicated." She pointed to the tapestry on the wall. The images had shifted again. At first, I thought the fabric caught a draft, but there wasn't one. It was the patterns in the weaving itself that were moving.

I saw a skyline, and a crest with a star. A sword, and angel's wings, and what appeared to be hieroglyphics.

"That was a gift to me from the Fates. She gave her own life to return it to me, to keep it from being destroyed or falling into the hands of an unscrupulous mortal."

"Is it that important?" I wondered out loud. It didn't really look special. I could almost chalk the images up to a trick of the light.

"This tapestry will show your future, if you let it.

Your destiny. Artifacts like this could turn the tide in battle."

"Is that— That's the tapestry the Athenians want. The one they wanted me to recreate."

"Yes. But contrary to what they might think, they have no claim on it. I won it, fair and square. Athena might be a goddess of strategy, but she's really not very good at poker."

"So you've had it all this time."

"The king of Atticus destroyed my temple because Athena told him there was power hidden there. She meant you, but you thought he wanted the tapestry. You know, that tapestry would only have shown its gift to certain people until you came. One touch from you, and it released the magic for all to see."

"I don't remember doing it."

"Evadne never knew precisely what she was doing. She merely did what she loved. The rest was mere happenstance, the result of Athena's blessing on Arachne and her family, before it was taken away."

"But what about me? Why am I here now, then?"

"You still carry that blessing, though it is part of you now. I can't take it away, nor Athena, nor any of her servants. Why don't you use it for something good?"

*Ah. Here we go. The sales pitch.*

"What exactly do you want?"

"Things are changing down here. For centuries, we were ignored. Powerless. But now, there are all of these new believers. Not just people reading the stories, but people who truly believe we exist, who give us prayers and offerings." She ran her hands along the frame of a painting. "I love these Wiccans, the neo-pagans that are popping up. They've drawn us out of the shadows, out of our forced hibernation. So many of us were fading into nothing, but now we are growing in power, all of us. Not just me, though they seem to like me quite a lot." She chuckled again. "Athena, Zeus, Hermes, and others, too—my dear Anpu, for example, and Isis, and dozens of others. We're coming back. But we aren't there yet. We're slowly taking back our duties, which is why I need you.

"You do not simply have Athena's blessing, but mine, as well. I bestowed it upon you when Evadne was a child, and it has stayed with you for all of this time. I confess, it has not served you as well as I hoped, but I think now, by using it in my service, for the good of all, you might be able to tame it a little.

"The world is full of ghosts, my dear. Send them to me, and I will reclaim a little of my power. And then, I can use it to help you."

"Help me how?" I asked suspiciously. Mostly, I just wanted to get rid of those stupid powers so Kelly and Traverse would leave me alone.

Hekate stood, going to stand behind her boyfriend. Anubis was putting the final touches on Big Ben. There were just a few loose pieces left on the table.

"I am one of the strongest gods in the underworld, and Anubis is one of the oldest. Together, we know of a way that can bring your dear Micha back to the land of the living."

"Why would you do that?" I asked, taken aback.

"Because I promised." The joy left her face for a moment. "When Evadne died, I offered her a reward as she passed through the underworld. Her only request was that she be reborn with her lover, that they may have a chance to live together as they had intended. I wanted to grant her wish, but Athena interfered, striking a deal with Hades. He dipped Micha's soul into the river Lethe, to prepare it for reincarnation, but instead of sending it to be reborn he merely sent it back to earth, destined to wander for eternity with no memory of his past, thereby separating the two of you for good.

"When I discovered his betrayal, I searched for Micha's soul. When I found it, it was too late for me to recover his memories, and alone I do not have the power to make him human again. I bound his soul to yours as a guardian, a spirit to protect you from future harm by Athena and her agents. The two of you are connected now, forevermore.

"I know your experiences with the gods have not been pleasant thus far, but I keep my promises. I will see to it that the two of you are reunited."

"But you just said you couldn't," I pointed out.

"Alone, no." She placed her hand on Anubis' shoulder again.

He looked up, puzzle complete. "I know of an artifact which might be helpful," he said, his voice as deep and rich as good earth. "It is forbidden where I am from, intended to raise a pharaoh from eternal sleep. The one it was made for, however, was vile, and it was hidden away to prevent him from attaining eternal life. Your love, he does not have a mummy?"

I shook my head. I didn't know what had happened to Micha's body, but I doubted that after a few thousand years I'd be able to find it, even on the off chance he'd gotten a proper burial after the battle ended.

"That is where I come in," Hekate said. She waved her arm, and the cardboard Big Ben vanished, replaced by a series of bones.

I gasped and stepped back. "Okay, creepy. Those are real? Oh my gosh."

Another wave of the long, pale arm, and the skeleton was gone, replaced by a piece of onyx, threaded with white. Closer inspection showed the white pattern was in the shape of a rib cage, the stone itself roughly the size of a spool of thread.

"This stone now holds Micha's bones, the last remaining pieces of him."

Anubis pulled a scroll out of somewhere I really didn't want to think about and offered it to me. "Place the stone inside the sarcophagus of the pharaohs. This will tell you the spells to say and how to use it."

"And you're just going to give it to me?" I asked, taking the scroll suspiciously.

Anubis shrugged. "Kate asked me to, and I have no use for it. Besides, no one knows where it is, so you'll have a bit of digging to do."

I couldn't tell if he meant that to be a pun or not.

"Like I said, I always make good on my promises. This one is just turning out to be a bit more complex and time-consuming than I initially thought. And we aren't doing everything." She tossed the stone in my direction.

I caught it reflexively, mostly to keep it from clocking me between the eyes.

"You'll still have to gather the other pieces. But don't waste any time. The sarcophagus will only work during the season of Akhet, when the stars are in exactly the right place. If you miss your window, it'll be another century before they line up again."

Anubis picked up the explanation. "He'll have to go into the sarcophagus at the start of the Khoiak ceremonies, at the time that Isis searched for the body of Osiris. He must stay there until the seventeenth day of Mechir, the day that he was resurrected."

"Sorry, my calendar doesn't come with an Ancient Egypt setting. When exactly is that?"

Anubis glared at me and I instantly regretted the

sarcasm.

"Come here," he ordered.

Timidly, I did.

"I want you to know I'm only doing this because Kate asked me to," he said. Then he planted a hot, dry palm on my forehead and started mumbling something in Egyptian.

When he released me, I was a little dizzy, with bright spots dancing in front of my head.

"There. That's all the help you'll be getting from me," he growled.

I stumbled back, catching myself on the armrest of Hekate's throne.

What they were offering me was something I hadn't thought possible. But there were a few things about it that bothered me. I'd read a lot of mythology, both in school and then also when researching the Athenians. There were two constant patterns.

"The dead don't come back. Not even Osiris could come back, and he was a god."

Anubis clearly thought I was asking too many questions. "Well, I never promised it would work," he scoffed.

"But it should," Hekate interjected. "You see, you're not resurrecting him in the strictest sense. You're creating a new body for his soul to reside in, which is different. And his soul isn't trapped in the underworld, so that's not a problem."

I ran my thumbs over the stone and the scroll, uncertain how to broach the next part. "I still… I don't understand why you would want to help me."

Anubis turned back to his puzzle, clearly giving up on me. I hadn't even seen it reappear.

Hekate came forward and looped my arm though hers

like we were old friends. "Let's just say I'm a sucker for a love story, then, and leave it at that. And it's not like we're getting something for nothing. Remember, you have your part of the bargain to hold up as well, if you're to get what you want. Which reminds me. Now that you've been here, and we have…an arrangement, others will be looking for you. Not just Athena. I can give you a little bit of protection, but it's only temporary." She stroked my hair, fingering a lock by my forehead. When she released it, I had a silver-white streak that matched the one in Micha's hair.

"It's not that I'm not grateful, or anything. It's just…I don't think I could forgive myself if I was here and didn't ask. My aunt… I mean, my mother…."

"Izzy. Yes. Unfortunately, that is Athena's magic. There's nothing I can do to break her curse, not as I am now. Perhaps, in time…but I'm sure you have other resources available to you, if you only look."

Oh, good. More cryptic answers. Just what I was after. I started to ask what she meant, but Anubis cut me off.

"Enough!" He snapped. "Mortals, always asking for more than they are given!" He held out his hand and blew me backward with a gale-force wind, straight into my own body.

***

I woke up on the floor, pretty much where I'd fallen. The cocoon was gone, and someone had opened the windows and brought in more light. I had to blink several times to process what I saw: women in Greek robes, being led out in handcuffs by uniformed police and plainclothes officers.

Micha was at my side in an instant. He shouted my name like a whoop of joy and threw his arms around my neck.

"Whoa, okay, I get it!" I said, shivering at his sudden icy touch. "What happened? Where were you?"

He released me reluctantly, disappointment on his face. I reached for his hand. He wasn't well suited to cuddling, but that didn't mean I didn't want contact. He smiled.

"I went for help. You'll never guess who I found parked out front."

I followed his line of sight to a tall redhead by the door, who appeared to be taking a head count. I couldn't see his face, but with the pinstriped suit and fedora, it could only be the crazy guy who had saved me from the train.

As if he could feel my eyes on him, he turned around. Nodding to a subordinate, he came over to join me, squatting on the mosaic floor so we were somewhat closer to eye-to-eye.

"What are you doing here?" I asked. The last thing I needed was a stalker, though if that stalker was a cop who was saving my life, I might make an exception.

"Making sure you don't get killed. Like I said, we've had our eye on you for a while. And on them." He nodded at the group of women being led out. "Usually these groups are pretty harmless, but every once in a while they go completely out into left field and we have to deal with them."

"Who is we?"

"The Night Shift. Cops for the paranormal set." He offered me a hand to help me stand.

"What's going to happen to them?" It wasn't like they could get a normal trial. Could they?

"They'll be held, questioned, and then dealt with," Ian said. I didn't like the way he said *dealt with*.

Glancing around, I realized the spiders had all vanished. "Wait—the spiders. Where did they go?"

Ian shrugged and scowled. "Scattered when we came in. The woman who was controlling them got away, along with one other."

"Kelly."

He nodded. "But don't worry; we've got teams out looking for them. Once someone shows up on our radar, they don't disappear easily. We'll find them."

"You have to find them. They have my aunt." I explained about Izzy and the spiders, and was surprised he took it in stride.

"Forcible transformation and enslavement of human beings? That right there will get them both put away for life," he said thoughtfully.

Now that everything was over, I could feel myself beginning to shake with fear and relief; I could turn this over to someone else now. It wasn't my problem. Someone else could take the reins. "You have to find her. I—it's complicated, but she's been missing and I don't know what to do and I can't tell my family or the cops and please tell me there's a way to turn her back!"

Awkwardly, Ian put a hand on my shoulder. "Don't worry about it, kid. We'll find them—and when we do, we've got the best sorcerers in the world working for us. They'll find a way to undo any harmful magic. In the meantime, you should go home. Don't say anything to anyone just yet. I'll do a little paperwork, see what we can't arrange about your mother."

"How did you—"

In response, he just winked. "I told you, I've had my eye on you for a while. You're an Adder. We'll take care of it."

Before I could ask any of the questions swirling around in my head, he vanished, melting into the controlled chaos around us.

I still clutched the black stone and the scroll. If Ian had noticed them, or my new hairdo, he certainly hadn't mentioned it or found it odd. Meanwhile, I was still getting used to the idea of dreams that connected to reality.

"Where did those come from?" Micha asked, hand on my waist, peering over my shoulder.

"Hekate. And Anubis." I examined my underworld souvenirs, unrolling a few inches of the scroll. To my untrained eyes, the sloppy symbols were complete gibberish, but the more I stared at them, the more they congealed into words—the result of Anubis' blessing. The first line of Hieratic dated the scroll to the reign of King Akhenaten, a secret project taken on by the hidden priests of Osiris in an attempt to restore the former king.

"Sounds cheerful," I mumbled.

"What do we do with it?"

"Research, for starters." I still had to find the sarcophagus, and figure out how it worked. And then there was the matter of Hekate's little errand. And trying to find Izzy.

And reversing the spell on her, however that was supposed to be done.

And somewhere in there, I would have to figure out how I was going to pay rent on Izzy's apartment, and something to tell my family.

And I hadn't even talked to my parents since Izzy's little bombshell.

Suddenly, tracking down an ancient, magical coffin and collecting souls for a goddess didn't sound so hard.

"Working for the gods is a good idea, right?"

One of Micha's eyebrows vanished behind his silver streak. "Please tell me you're joking."

"That's what I thought."

# Micha's Cowl

*Sturdy. Basic. There when you need it. And pretty damn cuddly, too.*

**Dimensions**: pattern as written is for an adult. Unstretched, cowl measures about 19" circumference.
**Needles**: Size 2.5 US/3 mm (DPNs or circular)
**Yarn**: 25g fingering weight yarn in 2 colors
**Optional Tools**: yarn needle, 1 stitch marker

**A note on yarn choice:** This pattern is appropriate for yarns ranging from light fingering-worsted. Using a thicker yarn and matching needle will obviously result in a larger cowl. The needle size and yarn listed are based on the averages for the yarn I used.

**To Begin:**
Cast on  92 stitches in Color 1. Join without twisting (place marker) and work in garter stitch for 4 rounds.

**Section 1:**
Using Color 1, *knit 2, yarn over, slip the next two stitches as if to purl. Knit slipped stitches together through back loop. Repeat until end of round.

**Round 2** and all even rows: knit.

**Round 3**: *knit 1, yarn over, slip next two stitches as if to purl, knit slipped stitches together through back loop, knit 1. Repeat until end of round.

**Round 5**: *yarn over, slip next two stitches as if to purl, knit slipped stitches together through back loop, knit 2. Repeat to end of round.

**Round 7**: *slip next two stitches as if to purl, knit slipped stitches together through back loop, knit 2, yarn over. Repeat to end of round.

**Round 8**: Knit.

**Section 2:**
Using Color 2, work in garter stitch for 5 rounds, beginning and ending on a purl round.

Repeat Sections 1 and 2 until cowl reaches desired length. End with Section 2, bind off.

**National suicide prevention hotline (US):
1-800-273-8255**
The Trevor Project (for LGBTQ youth)
1-866-488-7386

**Suicide prevention hotlines (Canada):
1-800-273-8255**
KidsHelpPhone Ages 20 Years and Under in Canada 1-800-668-6868
First Nations and Inuit Hope for Wellness 24/7 Help Line 1-855-242-3310
Canadian Indian Residential Schools Crisis Line 1-866-925-4419
Trans LifeLine – All Ages 1-877-330-6366

**National Domestic Abuse Hotline (US):**
1.800.799.SAFE (7233)
https://www.thehotline.org/

**Domestic Violence Crisis Text Line (Canada):
Text CONNECT to 686868**
https://www.crisistextline.ca/

# ABOUT SOPHIA BEAUMONT

Sophia Beaumont is an author of dark paranormal stories for young adults that deal with mental health, grief, and finding the magic in life.

Growing up isolated in rural Ohio, her childhood would not have been out of place as the plot for a Gothic novel, and provided the perfect backdrop for a developing author.

With a degree in fine art and art conservation, Sophia has a slight obsession with knitting, ghosts, and witches. In her spare time, she knits, crochets, sews, embroiders, and spins, among other crafty pursuits.

Her favorite thing about writing fantasy and paranormal is adding magic to every day events.

Sophia lives with her partner in crime and five little beasties that *might* be cats, or maybe just very fluffy genetic experiments gone wrong. She also writes Gaslamp mysteries for teens and adults as Sine Peril, and nonfiction (including knitting and crochet patterns) as Sheena Pennell. Together, they make up KnotMagick Studios.

**Find KnotMagick Studios Online:**
www.KnotMagickKnitter.com
Socials: @KnotMagick
Ko-Fi: Ko-Fi.com/KnotMagick
Youtube: @SinePeril

**If you enjoyed *Moreau House*, please consider telling others and writing a review.**

You might also enjoy these books by Sophia Beaumont:
*The Spider's Web (Evie Cappelli book 1)*
*The Ferrymen (Evie Cappelli book 2)*
*The Night Wars Collection* (with Missouri Dalton)
*Bind Off: The Evie Cappelli Bind Up* Omnibus
*All for One*
*Midnight Radio*
*Dru Faust and the Devil's Due*


Don't forget to look for these titles by Sìne Peril:
*Off the Rails*
*By the Grace*
*Colors in the Dark*

www.ingramcontent.com/pod-product-compliance
Lightning Source LLC
Chambersburg PA
CBHW051520150726
47997CB00001B/322